MAGIC AT THE END OF THE WORLD

BOOK 1

MICHAEL ONUFREYCHUK

CHAPTER

1

Living in the bunker was like losing every freedom and luxury, except for the right to learn and work. This was made worse by the leadership's overwhelming empathy, which I didn't resent, but cramming four times the recommended capacity into extreme survival mode forced everyone to live like sardines. The nuclear blast had occurred almost directly above our bunker, the resulting loss of comms, and the above-ground radiation sensors gave the military leadership the impression that the world was a complete loss. Ironically, this is what kept us safe from the worst of it.

After the bombs fell, all infrastructure was obliterated. While the initial global death toll wasn't as high, the true devastation came from billions fighting over the remaining resources. Being above ground became a death sentence. Governments struggled to maintain control and offer stability, forcing the political leaders, in nearly all the countries around the world, into hiding in well-stocked bunkers. These groups retained power by retreating while the world's population plummeted to a level they could once again subjugate.

The five years following the bombs were lawless, filled with extreme terror. When the world leaders finally resurfaced, despite their cowardice in hiding while billions perished globally, they were embraced by the survivors as their saviors.

Very few of our bunker inhabitants talk about how the world ended, and those who do share memories shy away from graphic details, sticking to the facts: "we traveled from here, Pilgrim X, Y, and Z died there." These types of stories are not exciting for a young mind. My people were mainly scientists and children of scientists. The first bunker we migrated from was under the US Air Force command. When the bunker's supplies dwindled, the isolated military leadership pushed out all the civilian personnel.

During our pilgrimage to our current home, a repurposed university, only the very lucky survived the journey. The creatures were massive and ferocious. Bears seemed to double and triple in size, insects were the size of birds. No rational theory can explain the near misses and close calls my family and the survivors experienced. While others seemed magnetized to destruction and were quickly decimated, my parents and close family appeared invisible to the hunt of the fallen animals. Out of 250 personnel, only 40 survived. My whole family, 9 in total, were among them.

The air was thick and humid, and at night, the sky shimmered with northern lights. Dust storms were frequent, and while plant life thrived, every plant we encountered was either carnivorous or poisonous. Vines would seek us out, and plants would shoot poisonous spore darts as we traveled. They ignored the 40 of us but quickly feasted on anyone else. However, the plant life in the fields leading up to the complex returned to normal—docile and quiet.

The massive university was surrounded by hastily constructed moats. I was seven years old when we arrived at the safe grounds of the university, which had been renamed Fort Patience. Located in Virginia, 400 miles from the nearest nuclear blast site, Fort Patience once an University now being used as a scientific research facility. The main structure had been repurposed, its lecture halls now serving as laboratories and administrative offices. The dormitory building housed all the personnel who lived and worked at the fort.

The defenses included several outer guard towers equipped with perimeter sensors, positioned 40 feet in front of a trench moat that encircled the facility. Behind the moat was a patchwork fence made of scrap metal, standing at least 16 feet tall. The old running track and football field had been repurposed into a helipad and maintenance area for the seven helicopters Fort Patience operated. Every inch of the grounds was meticulously maintained. The fort had an efficient ecosystem, producing its own food, water, and clothing, aided by the advanced technology developed there. Very little outside assistance was required to sustain the fort. Military protection was provided by the local government NEDU.

Life at Fort Patience was uneventful, boring, and routine. Days were filled with food, education, and brief free time before long shifts helping in the botany wing—digging, planting, and moving massive amounts of animal waste in and out of the gardens. The main objective of the botany wing, where my parents worked, was to grow food that could be easily transported and cultivated in harsh, radioactive zones. Thanks to their tireless efforts, food was plentiful for the fort's inhabitants. Once successful in the lab, the plants were flown by helicopter to remote sites, where other hazmat teams tested them.

I had never been to the test sites, but my parents would spend 2-month rotations away from me, totaling 6 months a year in remote sites. During this time I was left in the care of my Uncle Glorn. Regular transports of supplies would leave, and scientists would hurry off to the helipad in the morning and return in the evening. This is where I would go for drama and entertainment. The scientists would routinely arrive angry and deflated, and the technical discussions, however depressing, were still a nice reprieve from my scheduled life.

This went on for 3 years before my parents made a major discovery. The radiation was not the only factor as to why food plants would wither so aggressively in the high-radiation areas, so named High Tone areas because the detectors on the helicopters' radiation alert would go off the entire time on site. They called it Elemental "M," where the plants would turn gray within minutes of being planted. The plants would only survive after my parents made a discovery and created a shield, a type of force field object. This object was shaped like a dream catcher with rare stones around an unknown metal web. No one discussed how it functioned; it was a heavily guarded secret. All that was discussed was it is placed at the base of the plant and repelled Elemental "M."

After the success of the experiments and the rapid growth of the potato-like plants, my parents returned ahead of their rotation. They woke me in the middle of the night. The elder leaders interrupted our reunion with news the plant's force fields had to be moved immediately. Early warning sensors showed a large group of potentially hostile invaders moving toward the University grounds. The far guard posts only managed to send out an alert before their life monitors went blank and the comms played static. The defense leader hurried us off to the helipad; all basic equipment and gear were loaded before we arrived. We had no time to grab any personal belongings.

My uncle was the pilot, and we took off so quickly that as soon as my butt hit the seat, the engines were spooling up. A moment later, my head was forced into my lap as the helicopter lurched and shifted hard. My dad yelled, "Clear left!" and we were enveloped in a bright smoke. The helicopter's countermeasures activated on their own, still pushed into my seat, I felt heat and a pressure wave as an explosion came from the tail of the aircraft. Everything was in slow motion as we leveled off, and I caught a view of the University. The entire facility was burning bright blues and greens. If anyone survived the inferno, it would have been more than a miracle.

Still winded from the explosion or from the air blasting into the cabin of the helicopter, I snapped out of my shock to the "Pull up, pull up" of the Betty. "Terrain, don't sink!" My mind was a blur, I was unsure how long we were flying, but at that moment, the helicopter was falling fast. We didn't get away scot-free; the smell of dirty socks filled my nostrils—hydraulic fluid, I concluded—as pink liquid puddled at my feet. Moments before impact, my uncle reached back and grabbed my arm tightly. A buzzing sensation enveloped my whole body as we froze 10 feet from the ground and drifted through the falling tangled mass of moving metal and wildly turning gears. We phased through the top of the helicopter and landed gently 50 feet away.

My unblinking eyes strained for any remains but could not see any. Mom and Dad were nowhere to be seen. As we approached the wreckage, Uncle Glorn wasn't even startled, not breathing panickily like myself. To my surprise and shock, my parents were gone, along with all the gear we had onboard. Uncle Glorn knew exactly what I was thinking or perhaps what anyone might be thinking in this situation. He yelled, "They are safe, we need to get moving, we have no time for explanations."

Uncle Glorn and I had nothing—no food, water, or basic supplies. My clothes were singed and uncomfortably wet with oil and mud. The pace that we held was almost a sprint. We were heading west, away from the crash site and away from the newly visible tower of smoke now lit pink from the sunrise. I kept replaying the events leading up to the hurried hike. All of the magical moments like a shuddering frame by frame. I caught myself saying out loud, "My uncle is a witch." He snapped back, "A wizard actually."

Hundreds of questions floated into my mind. I blurted out, "Why are we running if you have magic?" My uncle replied without any change in pace, staring forward with a fixed gaze, "The invaders are sensitive to magic events; that is why they attacked Fort Patience."

"So Elemental 'M,' and the plants' miraculous growth was caused by magic?" I asked.

"Yes," he replied. "The charm was weak magic, but the scientists stacked all the charged stones for transport to the next site. This made the weak enchantments send out a sort of ping, and the magic sensitives were then able to hone into our location. Those buffoons at Fort Patience had no idea what they had and what myself and your mom and dad were carefully maneuvering, casting, and setting decoys during massive magic spells. All for them to just stack it haphazardly."

After what felt like an eternity or six hours of running, my uncle slowed to a walk. We were several miles away from the crash site. The sun was directly overhead, making it just after or around 12 pm. The forest that we were moving through opened into a large meadow. We finally stopped under a weeping willow on the edge of the grassy field. Surprisingly, I was not tired; three years of hard labor could be thanked for conditioning my endurance.

My uncle pulled out a small money bag, an ornate felt pouch with amethyst stones and a checkered pattern with a pewter-colored drawstring. It was no larger than a man's wallet. He opened it, and then his entire arm disappeared into the small pouch as he began to pull out food and water, then clothing for us to change into, and then a tent. My jaw must have hit the floor in shock, but I was not in any way ungrateful as my stomach was talking to me the entire morning and only got worse as the adrenaline diminished.

The food my uncle prepared was small, sawdust-like granola bars. They tasted like eating a wood sandwich—no taste but very filling. The bars were from a survival kit from an airplane, and the water was in silver-colored pouches. I ate without issue. Our situation didn't seem so dire now that my belly wasn't crying at me. After we ate, he started to set up the tent. It was not at all like a normal tent I was used to seeing. He didn't prop it up with poles, and the fabric looked like a pile of leaves. All he did was lay it out at the base of the tree and motioned for me to go in. I opened the zipper flap only to see a large domed interior.

I climbed down the steps of the ladder and walked to the cots while my uncle went to the farthest side of the interior to a makeshift comms terminal. It was noon, but I was dead tired. I just accepted that nothing seemed real. This all defied explanation, and I was just going along for the ride. What all can be possible, I wondered, as I fell asleep. This was both the worst and best day of my life.

CHAPTER

2

I woke up to my uncle shaking my arm, and then I heard what sounded like vehicles driving overhead. Uncle Glorn pulled me into the middle of the tent, hit a button in the center of an octagonal table, and the room shrank. The walls pulled in as he started whispering, "They are still tracking the magic. The smaller structure should be undetectable." He had made contact with Fort Patience. Most of the personnel, including our family, made it into the fallout bunker and survived the explosions above ground. The explosions in the botany wing were a self-destruct order by the leaders to conceal the work of the scientists. The invaders honed in on the helicopter and our escape; they didn't care about the rest of the populace at Fort Patience. The only loss of life was from the security forces in the armed tower postings, and now the magic sensitives were traveling overhead.

Our presence was hidden, and after the tent stopped shaking, we waited another hour. My uncle then hit the button on the table again. The room expanded to the same size it was before I was woken up. Telling time in the tent would have been impossible, but my uncle had a grandfather clock that chimed every hour. Three days passed like this, with my uncle at the comms console making plans with Fort Patience. All the aerial equipment was damaged, so rescue was out of the question, and my uncle was sure that the

University was unsafe for our return. He had other plans for me. At noon on the fourth day, he handed me a very old-looking book with Celtic inscriptions on the cover. I opened it, and the book was blank. He looked at me, both concerned and irritated. "Only our family magic can reveal the text." He tapped the cover with his left hand, and the cover text turned to English, and the pages started to fill with text. The cover read, "Levwick Family History of 75 Generations." He then explained that the book would only reveal information that is needed at the time it is needed. But since it would not unlock for me, I felt it was quite useless.

     "This is your first lesson. Reach out to the book with your thoughts. You will see a geometric shape floating in front of your eyes. You must manipulate it with your thoughts." As my uncle returned to the radio console, the pages and cover went back to the Celtic script. I sat there for an hour and was not able to see any shapes as my uncle had briefly described. In frustration, I tossed the book down on the table. A star shape flickered into my vision, and I was thrown into the air and against the domed ceiling. My uncle jumped up from the commotion I caused behind him, looked at me with a half-smirk, and declared, "That would be a defense spell," as I fell down and landed on the bed. I had no idea what I had done, but it followed my angered frustration. My uncle walked back over and picked up the book. It came back to life as he held it in his hands, and he started a half-sided conversation with it. The words he spoke were clear, but I only heard a heavy bass-like noise in response, muffling his conversation. He turned back to me and announced, "It's time you learn about your early ancestors." I got within two feet of the book, and I could see the text filling the page. But more alarming was the unintelligible bass noise changing into a high-pitched male voice, now clear as day, asking me, "Where would you like to start, known or unknown family history?" I rubbed my eyes while questioning myself if this was real or imagined. As I pinched myself I decided I should not be surprised by any new thing that occurs and blurted out, "Both."

The book, that called itself Jeeves—of all the most cliché names I could think of this was definitely in the top ten—exclaimed, "Excellent choice, young Sir Levwick." Sir? I thought, I had never been called sir in that tone, as if a regal gentleman were speaking to a royal monarch. The book spoke with an old English accent. "Okay, hold on to your socks, young man." I felt overloaded with the nuances of the tale the book wove.

My family traced its roots back over 1500 years. The Levwicks were among the first ten families to experiment with magic and form a structured method of manipulating it. Magic was not invented by our family; it has existed virtually since the dawn of time. Our family approached magic from a scientific point of view. They never learned how and why it happened, and it was an ever-exhausting mystery. The Levwick family's origin can be traced back to where France is now tracing their lineage back as far as 450s AD. During the summer of 455 AD when Rome was on the decline and the Celts were in the late Iron Age the Council of Ten Families met for the first time and established the rules of conduct for magic. The extent and power of magic were unknown, and the main use at this time was for survival, medicine, crops, and life extension. Using weaponizing magic in war was considered cruel, as one warlock could turn the tide of war. The weaker opponent could easily have 15 men virtually indestructible with their bare hands against a technologically superior force. Magic needed to operate to better the world, and seizing power was forbidden.

While listening, I could almost see the setting and faces of my early family. The images were foggy, and facial features seemed blurred. I was so enthralled that I didn't even notice Jeeves had stopped talking and Uncle Glorn was snapping his fingers in front of my face. "I received a coded message from your mom and dad. We need to pack up." He placed a plate of meal rations on the table along with a large gold amulet, 3 inches across, with a red ruby in the center, my name inscribed around the edge, and on a thick metal chain necklace. "Eat up" Uncle Glorn instructed.

As I ate the sawdust snack, he explained that this amulet would absorb my now-awakened magic and both conceal and store it while we traveled. He handed me rags and a grey cloak. "Do not remove the cloak. It needs to conceal the magic that is currently enveloping you." I looked, and around my hands, I saw a red glow with the faint star symbol rotating around my right hand. It was the same symbol I saw earlier when I performed a defense spell. Uncle Glorn continued, explaining, "Non-magic people cannot see this, but those who consume magic beings can. The amulet also needs to be hidden inside your shirt as it is a visual indicator for the rogue bounty hunters we may encounter during the next part of our journey. We will be passing through several settlements. We are pilgrims. Do not talk to anyone, as your educated accent will draw attention."

We packed up, and he placed all the supplies in the drawers at knee height that encircled the base of the walls around the domed structure. As we climbed the steps, the room bent and retracted to a point at my feet, and the room collapsed with each step. When we arrived on the surface, Uncle Glorn tucked the tent into his small pouch this still amazed me. The meadow was marred with deep ruts caused by the magi's vehicles. As we left the meadow we traveled along the path that the magic sensitives had created until we found an old and overgrown road. Uncle Glorn and I continued west, as we walked, I began to see the world through new eyes. Magic dust drifted through the air, shimmering with an angelic sparkle. The leaves were carefully tended and trimmed by tiny humanoid beings with translucent butterfly shaped wings. The fruit trees housed their cities, their dwellings were tiny homes with charming decorative doors built into the trunks of the surrounding trees. I could easily spend hours observing their small yet significant existence. In this miniature city, a thriving ecosystem buzzed with life—cobblers, smiths, and farmers busily moved their goods to the market.

Animals roamed the area, exchanging precious stones for small articles of clothing and children's toys for sale in the market. The land in this microcosm teemed with life, in sharp contrast to the gigantic fallen animals. I marveled at how this world had been invisible to me before. Some trees even bowed in my direction, their lower branches bending into an improvised curtsy.

Rats and other rodents wore tiny suit jackets and carried briefcases. Blue-collar rats donned mail carrier uniforms, their small embroidered bags holding both human-sized envelopes and animal-sized letters. The flowers on the trees and plants had beaming, smiling faces, and the mail-carrying rats bowed as we passed. The same vines I had earlier witnessed ensnaring people were now controlled being used as transport by small, fly-like creatures without wings. My uncle looked back at me as one 70-foot vine snaked past me on the opposite side of the road. "These are vine riders they domesticate the wild vines that are otherwise carnivorous. They call themselves Slyherders."

The slyherder, who was about 1 foot tall and looked like a common housefly but wearing a three-piece suit, blue shirt, grey tie, and a top hat, tipped his tiny hat in our direction, saying, "Top of the morning to you." My uncle chimed back, "And to you as well." Uncle Glorn stopped and looked at me with a deep grin. "You are taking all these changes rather well." He gestured for me to stay close. He chuckled saying, "Not all of the creatures we see today are this gentlemanly."

CHAPTER 3

My whole life had seemed so boring, mundane, catastrophically normal while all I was experiencing now was incredible. No words in my vocabulary, no words in the human language could express the joy I was feeling. I almost felt guilty that I was having a blast in a post-apocalyptic menagerie while the world and normal people had to endure a hideous and horrid existence. Uncle Glorn read my mind again. "This life gets both better and worse, unfortunately. I wish you had seen it before the fall." From my lessons at school and the elders' stories, the world seemed like a paradise, I had no such experience. I was born in a military bunker.

I spent the next three hours gawking in silence at all the alien—to me—plants and occasional strange animals. Uncle Glorn interrupted my stupor, pulled out his magic pouch, and raised his hand over the opening. Without a word, the family book popped out and changed from a small speck, expanding like a balloon inflating, to normal size. He handed me Jeeves as we continued to walk. "Time for your next lesson. Before I open Jeeves, I want you to tap your amulet and try to see the geo lock. As I explained earlier, reach out to it with your thoughts, and it should come to you without much effort since the amulet has concentrated your magic."

Doing as he instructed a 3D shape appeared in front of Jeeves. The lock had a decahedron in the center with three rotating rings which were inscribed with the English alphabet. The decahedron was revolving in the center; each of the points had a Roman numeral. I manipulated the points and connected the numerals I-VII, spelling out RECLUDO, which means unlock in Latin. The object flattened out onto the cover. I tapped the book, and Jeeves came to life and exclaimed, "C'était incroyable," which I understood as "That was incredible." Jeeves was still speaking in French. I stated politely, "Please use English, Jeeves" and he immediately started speaking English. "My apologies, Sir Levwick. Today's lesson will be on three of the ten families: the Levwicks, Dirtins, and Furtongues. These three families created a union due to their complementary abilities. Over 300 years, the Levwicks were appointed to selectively plan marriages to increase the potency of magical abilities. Levwicks possessed the ability to perform magic without magical equipment aids, e.g., staffs, wands, or casting rings. Dirtins had the ability to speak to plants, and Furtongues could communicate with feral animals. To prevent genetic pollution and defects, the traits were divided into three sub-families, and crossing was strictly controlled. Every 100 years, when crossing was authorized, children were born with the ability to hold all three powers. You and your uncle are both born from the crossing of families. Your uncle, being 110 years old, was from the previous crossing of the three sub-families. He possesses two of the three traits: the ability to speak to feral animals and cast magic without instruments. As for you, we only know of the ability to cast magic."

Uncle Glorn interrupted the lesson. I looked up from the book, and my uncle was standing near a large boulder. He motioned with his hand for me to leave the road. It was 7:30 p.m., and the sky was getting dark. "We have reached the first safe haven," he spoke in a whisper. "Do not be alarmed. This burrow is home to a large, friendly beast." We climbed the rocks around the large boulder entrance, jutting nearly vertically 10 feet downward, and the opening was 20 feet across. We slid down the rock face into the cave and were surrounded in darkness. Uncle Glorn snapped his fingers, and a small candle-sized flame appeared in the palm of his hand. I then heard a large bellowing breath coming from the back of the cave. With each breath, sand and dirt were kicked up into the air, obscuring the light cast by the flame. I heard a low, bass growl say, "I smell humans, I smell food, and a friend." Uncle Glorn called into the darkness, "Only friends approach."

"Is that you, Glorn?" a deep voice rumbled.

"Yes," Uncle Glorn replied. "Govlow, I want you to meet my nephew, Jamez."

 We slowly approached, and the large grizzly rose on his back legs. Uncle Glorn and Govlow shared a comical hug, mainly because my uncle was only as big as one of the grizzly's paws, and in the hug, Uncle Glorn almost completely disappeared into the Govlow's fur. Then it hit me: I could understand the conversation. I introduced myself and bowed in front of the massive grizzly bear. I wasn't sure why I bowed, but it seemed the only way to show respect at that moment.

Govlow spoke slowly, with each breath resonating in a very low, reverberating tone, "You honor me, young one. It is not necessary. I am bound to you and your family for my entire life in repayment to your uncle for saving my life during the Fiery Days. Settle into my fur and rest from your journey."

I lay down against Govlow's side. The slow rhythm of the bear's breathing and the warmth radiating from his fur contrasted starkly with the chill in the cave air, pushing me into a deep and restful sleep.

Upon waking, I noticed my uncle had pried the book from my grasp while I was still asleep and was deep in conversation with Jeeves. It was clearly a heated exchange; his hands were animated, and his body language was very expressive. He was breathing heavily, his back visibly rising from a distance. With a slam, he shut Jeeves and walked over to me. I was still nestled in Govlow's fur blanket. Govlow stood up as Uncle Glorn approached. "Time for breakfast," he announced before shuffling past my uncle and exited the cave.

I had no idea what had angered my uncle, as I had never seen a negative emotion from him in my entire life. When he slammed the book closed and turned around, his frustration seemed to vanish completely, as if he had hit a switch when he closed Jeeves. Uncle Glorn pulled out an old map and started to explain where we were and where we needed to go.

"We are currently in the state called Virginia, near the remnants of a city called Bedford. We need to travel to Louisville, Kentucky, to meet up with the Furtongues, who will then provide safe travel to Texas and a magic-friendly town full of our distant relatives."

Uncle Glorn and I packed up the few items we had outside of his magic pouch. The air was cool and crisp, and the forest noise was both loud and calming. At the mouth of the cave were large tree roots. Uncle Glorn used the roots to scale the rock face. When it was clear, he called down to me, "The way is safe." I climbed the wall using the roots, and my uncle reached down to pull me onto my feet. As he dusted the dirt and sand off my cloak, he paused for a moment and asserted with pride, "You have grown up so fast. We are all proud of you."

I didn't feel any different, and it had only been a few days since this adventure began. Uncle Glorn pulled Jeeves out from his pouch. "It is time for your next lesson." Reaching out to grab the book, I came up short as Uncle Glorn pulled it back and started to explain, "This time, I want you to try to reach out to Jeeves like before, but from a short distance. We can't have you staring down at the book, stumbling along, especially as we approach NEDU's city guard."

I focused and tugged hard to connect with Jeeves. To my surprise I heard him audibly speaking from where Uncle Glorn was holding him, twenty feet away. At the same time, I heard his voice inside my head, echoing his congratulations. It felt strange, as if I had pulled him into an inner, private conversation. A sense of unease washed over me, like I was being watched by someone hidden. I shrugged off the feeling, telling myself it was normal to feel abnormal. As the lesson concluded, my attention shifted back to the scenery around me.

The old, cracked highway wove and stretched into the distance. Five miles away, smoke could be seen rising above the treetops. The chill in the morning air gave way to heat and humidity as the sun climbed into view. The forest to our right and left was teeming with life; birds of all kinds were busy collecting and foraging. The road's edge and adjacent lands were covered in collapsed and dilapidated ruins, overgrown farms, swallowed-up farm equipment, and rusted old cars and trucks. The roadway had remnants of what looked like smashed and overturned vehicles, as if a large V-plow had moved through, clearing the disabled vehicles.

"Must have been one heck of a traffic jam," my uncle muttered, as if he were in mid-conversation with an invisible companion. I was slowly falling behind. Although I was of average height, my steps were half as long as my uncle's. Uncle Glorn was 6'5" and built like a linebacker from a pre-fall sport called football. It was comical watching him at Fort Patience, climbing into the helicopter every day, sitting like a large gorilla on a tricycle, barely able to fit. Uncle Glorn looked dark and weathered, with deep smile lines at the corners of his wide green eyes, a skinny nose, and thick lips. His hair was dark red and kept in a ponytail, while his beard was short and neatly trimmed, bordering on stubble length. Despite being 110 years old, he had the physique of a man in his mid 30s and appeared to be around 36. His large, muscular frame and dark, almost Mediterranean complexion with a hint of olive made his ethnicity hard to guess with so many contrasting features.

As for me, I had long red hair and blue eyes with gold flecks. I considered myself bland and ordinary: a small, pointy nose, average-sized lips, neither thick nor thin. At 5'0" and 10 years old, I had a skinny build and almost clumsy appearance, like a beanpole who had grown too quickly and couldn't quite control my limbs. The clothing Uncle Glorn had given me was two sizes too large, adding to my scrawny appearance.

CHAPTER

4

We arrived at the edge of the town around lunchtime. Even from a distance, I could see the city was well fortified with towering walls. "Traveling past the city of Bedford without going through would take two days," my uncle stated as he began pulling food from the magic pouch. I was pleasantly surprised to find wild berries, alongside the usual sawdust snacks, were on the menu today. The berries, like the animals were enormous; one blackberry was all I could eat in a single sitting.

After lunch, Uncle Glorn stood up, dusted off his shirt, patted me on the back, and assured me that everything would work out. He handed me some local ident papers and waved his hand over the small booklet, causing the photo to change to a current, wide-eyed version of myself. "I wish you had warned me," I remarked.

Uncle Glorn smiled, "Yes, it's not the most flattering expression, but not unlike what other emotions of the locals would display given the state of the world. As I warned you before, do not speak until you can mimic the local accent."

He packed up our makeshift campsite, and we stepped back onto the roadway. As we approached the massive walled archway, the rusted metal blocks, which had looked like large toy blocks from a distance, now appeared even more imposing up close. Each block was two stories tall, and the archway stretched upward with ten blocks, making us feel as tiny as ants. Camera equipment and loudspeakers surrounded the archway, flanking the massive metal double doors.

Uncle Glorn approached the comms box, inserted both our idents, as a muffled voice came from the loudspeaker, "State your business, citizens 2K31 and 2K99." Uncle Glorn replied, "Rest, shelter, transient passage." A slot opened, and a transfer for ten days was approved. Inside the slot were maps, a code of conduct, local laws, emergency service locations, and curfew regulations. The concrete threshold shook, and the wall made a heavy, threshing sound before sliding open just wide enough for Uncle Glorn to squeeze through sideways.

The city smelled of wet, dirty socks or a wet dog wearing dirty socks. The air was thick and damp, and the smell was overpowering. Until now, my dwellings had been clean; my work around plants had exposed me to manure and hearty plant smells, with a clean feeling and a geothermically generated AC system at Fort Patience. Here in Bedford, it was stiflingly claustrophobic with too many people.

The streets were crowded with small shops of varying sizes. The people were dirty, and there was little color on the streets. My clothing matched the city's dreary atmosphere perfectly. The most alarming sensation was a magical weight pulling at my soul, creating a very bad vibe that was hard to pinpoint and even harder to explain. No one in the crowd had a smile, and the bustling bystanders looked like they were in a trance as they carried out their almost robotic chores, as if they had repeated the same routine a thousand times, leaving defined tracks on the cracked, uneven asphalt. I did not like this place and yearned to be free from its depressive gloom. Ten days seemed like an eternity. I heard Uncle Glorn's voice in my head, like an internal dialogue. "I'm unsure how you managed to access this ability without training, but you're literally yelling these experiences in magic tongue. I'll explain it later. Please take your left hand off the amulet; magic sensitives might detect the weight of this inner dialogue. You don't know how to whisper in magic tongue yet."

Looking down and saw that I was clutching the jeweled amulet so tightly that my knuckles were white. My disgust for my surroundings had inadvertently triggered a new ability. I really had no idea what I didn't know about magic.

We walked through the crowd for two hours until Uncle Glorn motioned for me to follow him to a large mural wall. He walked towards the wall, reached back and grabbed my arm, and as he approached the mural, all but his hand disappeared into the grey and black painting. I stepped into the wall, and everything went black. A small light appeared, like at the end of a train tunnel growing closer and then blinding me.

We emerged into a small, bright, and sunny courtyard with a hanging garden. "Welcome to Bedford's safe house, called the 'Cubby Hold Garden.' I heard you earlier; no, we will not be here for ten days. We had to use this safe house instead of taking the trolley out of the city as I had planned. Your noise may have alerted the magic sensitives, out of an abundance of caution we will hide here for two days. During this time, I've decided a magic introduction is absolutely necessary. This space we're in is a pocket world. No level of magic will be felt in the city of Bedford. Before you ask why we don't just live in a pocket world, only one wizard was able to create these pocket worlds, and the concentration of magic can only exist with an equal and opposite amount of negative energy. An entire city was needed to keep this small space in equilibrium."

Cubby Hold Garden was not exactly small. The

outer walls were covered with rose vines, extending 100 feet from the center of a round table. Around the table were eight archways forming an octagon. At each archway was a rectangular table. The arches were adorned with a rainbow of glowing geometric shapes and hieroglyphs. The stone was flat and smooth with a polished sheen, as if carved from a solid block of granite. I couldn't stare at the text for long before it became blindingly bright.

"These are the room's bindings," my uncle interjected, breaking the silence as I observed the structures. "These bindings keep this world turning, so to speak. Do not pull on any of the loose threads."

I didn't fully understand what that meant, but I didn't dwell on it. My entire imagination was focused on the telepathic communication I had accidentally performed. What else could exist?

Uncle Glorn sat down at the central round table and beckoned me over. He gestured in the air, and one of the large stone chairs slid back for me to sit in. "It's time for a ground-level magic lesson. We'll start with the basic parts of the spells you've already done. First, you need sufficient power, a recipe, and the right activating phrase. The language was programmed into you at a very young age. Each magic family has its own method for activating spells. The same magic may be produced, but the approach differs. This procedure was mastered by each family over 700 years ago and lasted 180 years in what was like an arms race to develop and control magic for the families. Most basic magic is mapped, but much is still unknown. Old magic, like this safe house construction, has been lost or is kept hidden and safeguarded, like the pioneering work your parents were involved in. Anything is possible within the bounds of Magic Law Works, also known as Mag Work Iks."

1. **Absolute Death is Final:** This occurs when the

brain ceases functioning and the soul is no longer imprinted into it. Reanimation is possible
but accelerates the decay of the corpse, making it
 a short-lived process where the shell usually turns to dust within three days, depending on the time of absolute death and the complexity of the magic or skill involved.

2. **Not Everything Lasts Forever:** Most things wear out, decay, or break, with the exception of living magical artifacts. These artifacts tend to strengthen and develop personalities, and in rare cases, they become sentient beings. For example, Jeeves is a magical being and is alive. (Things created without a balance of magic fail; it is an absolute rule.)

3. **You Can't Live Forever:** The longer you extend your life, the more difficult it becomes to cast extension spells. Immortality is not possible.

4. **Nothing is Free:** Creating something requires a loss. Magic essence destroyed in a family is redistributed among the surviving members. For example, our family once numbered about 1,000 members across eight generations prior to the fall. Now, only 10 members remain.

Now, onto the nitty gritty: Be cautious with the amulet and do not touch it unless you intend to use it. With only 10 family members remaining, magic is calling to you. You will have great difficulty avoiding using magic, also when you flex your abilities you will not be able to control the intensity. A small push spell in your novice state could have unintended consequences. Try to manage your emotions and avoid hyper-focusing on a spell as you cast it. The longer you dwell on the spell the more power will be infused into the casting."

Uncle Glorn paced as he delivered this monologue. I

understood the introduction to the laws and was confident I could avoid touching the amulet. My mind buzzed with questions, but I resisted asking them. Uncle Glorn stopped and turned to me. "I can see you want to practice some of the magic you've learned."

Nodding eagerly I blurted out, "Magic tongue, please."

Uncle Glorn sighed, his body language softening. "Alright," he murmured as he returned to the chair next to me. "I'm not a fan of this communication method and intend to use magic tongue only in rare and special circumstances. Be warned: speaking into non-magical minds can have disastrous consequences, one being death the lesser side effect being madness. Let's begin. Grasp your amulet."

Barely containing my excitement I grabbed it eagerly. "Now, think of your words and wait for the Latin word to fill your mind. Think the spell while looking at me. As soon as you see a visible static shock strike my temple, stop dwelling on the Latin word and convey the message, feeling, or abstract image. You'll need to lower your tone, Jamez," my uncle instructed, doubling over in pain.

I tried sending a memory—a fond moment of my mom rocking me and singing a lullaby. The image appeared vividly at first but faded as I pushed the thought away. Uncle Glorn was recovering in his chair as I repeated the process as instructed.

My uncle exclaimed cheerfully, "That was perfect! It played out in my mind like a short movie. Perfection!"

After Uncle Glorns praise I got up, walked over to him, and confessed that sending words was difficult. Uncle Glorn replied, "We could be too close; your voice may be better suited for long-distance calling." He chuckled at my puzzled expression, as I had no idea what long-distance calling was.

CHAPTER
5

The light was an actual sun in the pocket world's miniature sky. Neither of us noticed the passing of time and were equally surprised when the sun began setting over the outer wall, casting a beautiful red glow across the archways. The air was cooling off, and a light breeze was becoming noticeable on the far side of the room. Stars began to appear in the sky, and the last of the sunlight was replaced by a calming blue moonlight that filled the space. This place was a work of art, the magic exquisite. The level of true-to-earth astrological detail was not necessary for a simple safe house.

Uncle Glorn, now slumped over the table, snored like a large gentle teddy bear. He had not elaborated on any aspect of this space and how it worked, but I was captivated and eager to learn more. When morning came, I would ask so many questions that his head might explode—or, if necessary, I could threaten to use magic tongue should he resist.

I found a large patch of mossy grass and lay down to sleep. A wet, scratchy sensation on my face woke me from my sleep. The small sun was blurry in my morning groggy vision, just rising above the rose-covered outer walls. Looking around, I saw nothing. I laid my head into my folded hands and started to doze back off when the wet, scratchy sensation returned to my forehead. The unexpected sensation jolted me awake as I looked around I still saw nothing, and only heard Uncle Glorn's deep, loud snores.

Repositioning my robes, I prepared to walk around the room. As I leaned back to stretch, my hand brushed against my amulet, at that moment, a small creature flickered into view in front of me. Being startled fully awake I felt the wet, scratchy sensation on my cheek again. When I grabbed the amulet the creature appeared an inch away from my face, licking me. I jumped back, wide-eyed, taking in the sight of the creature.

It was clearly friendly, but what was it? Unsure if I was hallucinating, I reached out slowly with the hand that wasn't grasping the amulet. The fox-sized creature moved past my hand and snuggled under my neck. Its scaly, hot tail scratched my neck as it turned in circles several times before settling halfway inside the collar of my shirt. The creature had the scales of a lizard, the face of a fox and was only visible to me when I touched the amulet.

The animal, if I could call it that, was sweet and friendly. It muttered in gibberish phrases not in full sentences: "friend, friend, alone, friend, lonely, need friend." I was frozen in place, not out of fear but simply at a loss for what to do next. Instinctively, I started petting it.

"Yes, I am a friend." The creature let out a loud snuffing sound, followed by a small fireball. I scoffed, laughed, and thought, My first dragon-like creature—what do I do now? I felt less alone in that moment and forgot all my questions. Now, I was wondering what this pet's name was. I must have been speaking out loud because the dragon replied, "Argileous."

"Okay, Argileous," I asked, "what are you?"

"I don't know. I am Argileous. I woke up in the tunnel and then removed the sweat taste of salt from your face," the creature replied.

Looking over Argileous, I noticed a large raised bump on its head. "I will do my best with you," I avowed.

At that moment, my uncle lifted his head and murmured, "We haven't even had breakfast yet. Please save your talks with Jeeves until later when I'm done sleeping." He glanced at me, with the dragon in my lap and my face looking like I'd been caught with my hand in the cookie jar. He squinted at me, whispering, "It's not a big deal," before going back to sleep. He hadn't noticed my new pet, and I was relieved. I expected he would make me leave it behind when we left.

I whispered to Argileous, "May I call you Argil?" The dragon smiled and nodded.

"Also, I'd like to speak to you in magic tongue. Fair warning, I'm very rusty." Argil looked back at me with a confused expression.

"I guess you don't know what magic tongue is," I remarked.

Argil shook his head. "I'm sorry, if this hurts tap my hand, and I will stop." I sent a simple sentence, "What do you eat?" as quietly as I could.

Argil replied in my internal dialogue, "Delicious face salt mixed with your magic aura and anything on the ground that makes red water, I think."

"You mean animals?" I asked.

"Yes," Argil replied. "Any small thing that fits in my mouth."

"I have no idea how to take care of you, Argil," I admitted.

"Take care?" Argil exclaimed loudly in my head. "No, I hunt. No one cares for Argil."

With that, I felt a bit less overwhelmed. "Why are you invisible?"

"Argil is not invisible. Argil can see all his limbs, tail,

wings, and more," the dragon replied.

I asked again, more specifically, "Why can't people around you see you? I can't see you without my amulet in hand."

Argil cocked his head to the side like a small dog hearing a familiar phrase. "I don't know why," he replied. "Please care for me. I'm lonely and lost."

I asked myself - he fends for himself, so what's the worst that could happen? For reasons unknown to both Argil and myself, he was invisible. The next question was best directed at Jeeves.

I whispered, "Jeeves, can you hear me?"

Jeeves replied, "Yes, Sir Levwick. I have been listening to you and your baby dragon this entire time."

"Why is he invisible?" I asked without hesitation and before Jeeves could respond I added, "Why can I only see him while holding my amulet?"

Jeeves continued, "To answer the obvious mystery first, he has lost his memory. As for the invisibility, these breeds of dragons control light around themselves; they cancel out its effects. I'm afraid no one, to my knowledge, has ever encountered them up close. It could be that your yelling in magic tongue in the city streets, coupled with his memory loss, led him to follow you."

A loud BANG... BANG....BANG echoed inside the courtyard. Uncle Glorn jumped up. "Something is impacting this world!" he yelled as the walls shook and flower petals fell to the ground.

Another, even louder BANG resonated. Without hesitation, Uncle Glorn ran over to me, grabbed my arm, and pulled me toward one of the archways. I couldn't make out the flurry of spellwork at the archway; the shapes blurred together. A portal opened, and we jumped through it.

We landed—or slid—through thousands of parallel

lines of bright reds and greens, finally standing on a set of train tracks with Bedford a great distance behind us. I was so rigid with fear that I didn't even notice Argil constricting around my neck, almost choking me. I tapped the lump around my neck and whispered, "Relax," in magic tongue. Argil lessened his grip, and his breathing pulsing body returned to his usual calm state.

Uncle Glorn looked at me without explanation. I knew we needed to run immediately. I wondered who or what could have tried to breach Cubby Hold Garden. Who was pursuing us? Who even had the ability to break through a magical barrier? Could they follow us through the portal? How far behind were they? All these questions fueled my sprint to keep pace with Uncle Glorn.

We ran through the cool morning air, with the leaves changing into beautiful autumn gold, which seemed odd for June. We ran along the tracks for two hours until we heard a train approaching from behind us. My uncle, very fond of pulling me by the arm like a small backpack, yanked me off my feet and into a bluff beside a large post with a hook and lights. It looked like an old road crossing, but the path was so overgrown that it resembled a small foot trail.

Uncle Glorn crouched in the bushes, pulling down a low-hanging pine branch to hide his large silhouette. As the train cars passed, he spotted an empty train car with its sliding door open. Almost comically, I was flung through the air into the open train car and landed in a pile of hay that horses were actively eating from. Nothing made me feel smaller and more inadequate than being tossed around like a sack of potatoes by Uncle Glorn. At least it was a break from running— I reasoned— as I exhaled the air that I had acquired while I flew toward the train car moments earlier.

We rode the train in silence until stars began filling the night sky. My uncle hung out of the train car, gazing up at the sky. After ten minutes, he turned, walked toward my hay pile, slumped down beside me, and wished me a happy birthday this would make it October 18th.

"Time moves faster inside the pocket world," he explained. "The constellations are five months ahead of when I last looked at the night sky."

"It looks like it's mid-October now," he continued, noting the golden leaves. The explanation was perplexing and the world now looked like winter was just around the corner.

Argil whispered, "Happy Birthday."

Eleven years old at last, I thought.

CHAPTER
6

Sitting in the train car, I mulled over all my questions. I needed to condense my message and eliminate unnecessary words. An idea struck me: I would create a thought picture with all my burning questions and send it to Uncle Glorn like a picture book.

Uncle Glorn was sitting across from me, his legs hanging out of the train car opening, holding Jeeves in one hand. I assumed he was planning our next step of the journey. Given that we had lost five months, who knows how much had changed?

I had three main questions:

1. Where are my parents? I visualized a picture of my mom and dad with a map and a giant question mark.

2. Who was chasing us? Were they wizards? I pictured a cloaked figure with a large staff sending a dramatic fire bolt at the mural from Cubby Hold Garden.

And the last burning question was....

3. Can I have a pet? I briefly recounted how I found the dragon and apologized for not alerting him sooner.

I was ready to send it. With the images in my head, I called over to Uncle Glorn, "I need to talk to you, sir." I sputtered sheepishly, "May I send it to you in magic tongue?"

Uncle Glorn agreed and turned his attention away

from Jeeves. I sent the message, and within two seconds, his expression changed from concerned to a soft smile. "Message received," he asserted and returned to his conversation with Jeeves. I felt more than a little irritated, as I stewed this was more important than whatever he was doing.

After an hour, Uncle Glorn shut the book, got up, and walked over to me, kneeling in front of me. The hour-long wait had already frayed my nerves, so I blurted out the only question of the three that mattered, "Where are my parents?"

Uncle Glorn placed his left hand on my shoulder, Jeeves still in his right hand. "They are safe but stuck. Jamez, do not be alarmed and save comments until I have explained everything. Moments before the helicopter crash, your parents and I spoke in magic tongue and decided with your parents' approval to move them into Jeeves. They are neither dead nor alive."

He opened Jeeves to the last page, which showed a picture of my mom and dad sitting in the helicopter, with flames at the edges fading to white where air and sky would have been. "They are in limbo, and I lack the skill to remove them safely. That is the real reason we need to travel to Texas. The world's oldest wizard has set up a school there."

"They are stuck?" I exclaimed out loud.

"Yes," Uncle Glorn declared, his tone serious, his eyes unblinking.

"Why can't you free them?" I blurted out.

"This process is only performed on our family members shortly after death to preserve our family's knowledge. That is why Jeeves knows so much of our history and why he gained sentience. No one living has ever been added to the book. I do know they are intact and separate from Jeeves, as I had a very real argument with them at Govlow's den. They wanted to speak to you then. For your focus on survival in the moment, I thought it best to spare you from this knowledge. Looking back, perhaps it was a bad decision, as I have not heard from them since. But the good news is that with the comms equipment, I contacted my source at the school, and he is confident they are not gone."

I was shocked but relieved. This news was better than an "I don't know," and the idea of speaking with them through Jeeves was comforting. However, it raised the stakes: we were all that stood between four family members and death if we failed. It also explained why my uncle, a powerful wizard, was avoiding combative exchanges.

"Onto your next question," Uncle Glorn continued, "The magic sensitives' leadership desperately wants to destroy your parents' discovery. The discovery that is in Jeeves—who they are by name is a mystery. Last but not least, you found a gypsy dragon, or rather, it found you and brought us the uninvited guest. Given that, the dragon is an infant and astronomically, infinitesimally rare. No scientist in our family has been able to study them."

Uncle Glorn was more excited than I was, like a kid describing their favorite thing until the listener runs away.

"Yes," Glorn imparted finally, "but I would not be able to stop an invisible dragon even if I tried. Well, where is this elusive friend you have made?"

I could feel Argil shivering under my chin. "He seems a bit shy; he is wrapped around my neck."

Argil groaned and spoke in magic tongue, "Don't tell him that."

I asked Argil, "Please appear for my uncle. You can trust him."

Argil reluctantly agreed, "If you're sure he's safe, I trust." His body became visible, his scales flipping as he came into view.

Uncle Glorn, still kneeling, was in tears as he spoke. "I have never seen anything like this! What an incredible creature."

Argil bowed and spoke aloud, "I am Argileous, but Jamez calls me Argil."

"A pleasure to meet you, Argil. It is an absolute honor," Uncle Glorn responded with equal civility.

"Argil has no memory prior to Cubby Hold Garden," I told Uncle Glorn.

Uncle Glorn examined Argil with a concerned expression. "We must treat that head injury. Argil, may I look closer?"

Argil agreed but tightened his tail around my neck. He spoke in magic tongue, "Promise I'm safe?"

"Of course, Argil," I replied.

He released his grip and slid down to the train car's wooden floor between Uncle Glorn and me. Uncle Glorn slowly reached into his pouch, pulling out a small animal health kit. Moving carefully, he cleaned the wound around Argil's head bump and applied a healing lotion. "This should aid in healing."

Argil was stiff, his limbs coiled like a spring ready to run. Uncle Glorn announced, "All done," and pulled a live mouse out of his pouch like how you get a lollipop from a doctor after each visit. Argil grabbed the tail, flipped the mouse into the air, and swallowed it whole. "Mmm, Argil loves little snacks."

Argil climbed back onto my shoulder, then disappeared from view as he crawled through my collar and rested on my lap under my cloak. "Glorn nice, thanks for the snack," he purred, then snored and fell fast asleep.

"Okay, now that pleasantries are in order, we can discuss the next part of our journey. We will face the most challenging part of our journey, more challenging than anything we have faced up til now" Uncle Glorn proclaimed. "We are approaching the DMZ checkpoint, and I need to explain the political environment we find ourselves in. Prepare yourself; this will be boring but crucial for our survival."

Uncle Glorn pulled out a map of the old USA. "In green is Canada. After the fall and collapse of the USA, several West Coast states seceded and joined Canada, one of the few countries not affected by nuclear war. The Republic of New Texas, known as RONT, formed with the bulk of US military equipment, and Texas assumed control of the USA. All states that wanted the USA to endure joined RONT.

The entirety of the East Coast rebelled against RONT's formation, seeking to control the USA due to the old District of Columbia and the location of the historic White House. The New England Democratic Union (NEDU) has the highest number of MAGI, the magic sensitives, and they have a firm grip inside the NEDU government. MAGI are a fanatical, near-cult-like body that hunts down magical beings, human or beast. They are brutal cannibals who eat what they catch. They can see magic creatures because they've consumed them. No one knows who the leaders are, when or how they first gained sensitivity to invisible magic creatures. It's clear that one of the ten families heavily influenced the creation of the MAGI. The MAGI were ordinary people with no magical abilities before the fall. And now, the MAGI are the ones chasing us."

I had little interest in Uncle Glorn's briefing and fought to keep my eyes open. It was very late, and my eleven-year-old attention span was drifting. Uncle Glorn noticed and clapped his hands near my nodding head.

"Jamez, this is important," he snapped.

Jeeves chimed in, "It is nearly 2 AM; rest would be prudent for both of you."

Uncle Glorn sighed and conceded. "Fresh minds will take in this information better. We shall continue in the morning."

I hated the idea but had no energy to argue. I slid onto my side and fell asleep in the hay.

CHAPTER
7

It felt like the moment my head hit the hay, I was rising into a large meadow as if I had fallen through the floor into a world on the other side. Instead of the moonlit train car, I was now in a bright, sunny meadow. The rhythmic clack-clack of the train was replaced by beautiful bird songs, and the sun's warmth was comforting. All the previous uncomfortable sensations from the clothing I wore during my week-long journey were gone. Calm, comfortable, and clean, I got to my feet to explore the dreamscape. The sky was a vibrant blue with large white fluffy clouds, and the meadow was full of every type of plant I had seen and read about.

Something felt off, as if my eyes and brain couldn't fully process this location. For a dream, I had a surprising amount of control. I walked around the field, which was bordered by giant stone pillars resembling Stonehenge. Behind these towering stones was a wall of smoke that reached beyond my sight and faded into blue hues.

A familiar voice echoed through the field. "Jamez, Jamez, Jamez." I turned toward the sound and saw two silhouettes in the middle of the field. As I walked closer, their faces came into focus. I started running, faster than I ever had. My mom was wearing work coveralls, her red hair long and brushed by the wind, her green, caring eyes, red lips, and big smile clearly visible. My mom, sturdy at 5'5", never wore makeup, and her earthy fragrance filled the meadow.

My dad stood beside her, his weathered face adorned with a thin mustache, classically styled wide and curled up at the ends. His brown hair was neatly combed to one side, and he wore wire-framed glasses that rested on the tip of his large, round nose, giving him an intelligent look. His light grey eyes, resembling granite, reflected a sharp focus. He had a slim, athletic build, standing at 6'2". Permanent marks from a full-face mask creased the skin around his chin. Despite holding a position that included a generous clothing allowance, he preferred dressing in very basic colors, often choosing outfits nearly identical in color and style—grey overalls paired with a white polo shirt and light brown leather boots. They were still in the same clothing with name tags on their breast pockets reading Dr. Julia Levwick and Dr. Jeremy Levwick—exactly as they were on the day of the crash.

They reached out to me as I ran faster and jumped into their open arms for the best, tightest hug ever. The hug felt timeless. "We are so proud of you, Jamez." my dad marveled. As I turned to my mom she began "Now that your eyes and mind are open to magic, you can meet us in your dreams. Yes, this is real; yes, this is a dream." Dad continued, "You are full of surprises, Jamez. Meeting here the way we are has never been done before, just like so many firsts for you."

Jeeves's voice cut through the moment, "Wake up, Jamez. Wake up." I fought to stay but mom, dad, and the meadow began to fade. My parents reassured me "We are here, we are with you. We love you," they both affirmed. Then Mom's voice changed to Uncle Glorn's. "It's time to wake up."

The train started to slow down. Uncle Glorn was hastily placing food on my lap. I gulped it down as quickly as I could.

"We are approaching the DMZ," he asserted. "I hope you remember some of what I explained last night because we won't get another chance to discuss it."

What a relief, I thought. Just then, Jeeves spoke into my head with magic tongue, "I am extremely impressed with you, Sir Levwick. You created a pocket world inside my very pages to meet with your parents. Truly astounding! You may just be a savant, young sir. I am here if you need a refresher of your uncle's briefing."

"No, thank you, Jeeves. Once was enough," I responded in magic tongue. I didn't mind it too much, but I couldn't stand repetitive information. I could recall the important parts… maybe.

The train made a long turn and began to pick up speed again. Uncle Glorn threw me over his shoulder as the DMZ came into view. He jumped from the speeding train which was now traveling at double its velocity. We landed with a crash into a withered brier bush, then rolled into a ditch. Heavy machine gun fire erupted from both sides of the train, which was moving recklessly fast, almost a blur through the hail of gunfire. I didn't dare move as I lay in the muddy grass beside the tracks, watching the train speed out of view and then out of earshot.

The gunfire eventually subsided, and the area went eerily silent—no birds, bugs, beasts, or people, just deafening quiet. Uncle Glorn moved slowly, pulling out the tent and its leaf-like camouflage as if unrolling a rug. He opened the flap to reveal a ladder. Uncle Glorn motioned for me to enter with his face low to the ground, his chin submerged in mud. I slithered into the opening and fell into the tent's octagonal structure, hitting each step with the side of my face, my arms spread out in front of me, futilely trying to grasp at the steps to slow my fall.

At the bottom, I watched as Uncle Glorn gracefully rolled in, tucking his legs perfectly to catch the top rung of the ladder and easily lower himself down. It was still early in the day, around 9 AM. I was mentally exhausted from the adrenaline and stress. I felt disgusted, caked in mud, the icing on my scratchy, salt-infused garments. My socks and shoes were creating blisters and heat sores. I grabbed a sheet off the bunk and removed all my soiled clothes.

Without missing a beat, Uncle Glorn handed me new clothing—this time, a more traditional dress uniform with a tie and jacket. "After you're dressed, I'll teach you how to assemble the Windsor knot for your tie," he remarked.

In all the excitement, I had forgotten about Argil. I jerked around to find him still near the ladder, covered in mud from head to tail. Just in time, he shook wildly, sending mud flying in every direction before disappearing from view as the last droplets of muddy water flew off his body. "All clean," Argil chirped in my direction. I wished it were that easy for me at the moment.

Uncle Glorn pulled out Jeeves and sat down at the comms equipment. He looked back at me and instructed, "Be sure to use the portable shower and clean up the mess." A portable shower? I hadn't noticed one before. Sure enough, on the backside of the ladder was a water bag, a small showerhead, and an absorbent pad on the ground. I used only two gallons of water, but it was the most magical thing I had experienced that day. Finally, I was clean too. I used the shower water and wet rags to clean up Argil's mess.

I had dreamed of owning a pet my entire life, and I was finally enjoying the chores. Maybe someday taking care of Argil would feel like a chore, but right now, I was elated to have a menial task for my friend or pet—although I wasn't sure which, as my idealized view of having a pet didn't include one that could talk.

Uncle Glorn spent only an hour at the comms before returning to the table. "I have some good news and some sour news. The good news is that the Furtongues will meet us at a city closer to the DMZ. The sour news is that we need to cross tonight. I haven't figured out a way through the mines and tripwires, not to mention the trigger-happy gun emplacements on either side of the DMZ. It's 100 meters of flat land, 131 steps at your stride, with obstacles and razor wire meant to slow intruders to an inch by inch crawl"

Argil started tapping my leg and spoke in magic tongue. "I can cross. I did cross 30 suns ago."

I thanked him, and an idea hit me. I asked Uncle Glorn if I could suggest a dumb idea. He agreed, "Something is better than nothing. Let's hear it."

"Can we fit in your pouch, carried by Argil?"

Uncle Glorn considered this. "He's light enough not to set off the mines, and he's invisible… yes, this could work. However, the pouch is a free space, so it could feel like we're suspended in air but pressed against all the items stored inside. It would at least be uncomfortable, at worst painful."

I interrupted, "Argil tells me he crossed it only 30 days ago."

"You need to ask Argil if, after he gets to a safe place, he will be able to reach into the bag and retrieve us, as we won't be able to exit on our own. If this fails, we'll be stuck inside a small bag until we starve."

I relayed Uncle Glorn's message, but Argil was already listening and replied out loud, "I hear, I do, I will dig you and Jamez out if you bring more tasty treats from the bag. I'm hungry." Uncle Glorn glanced at his pocket watch it was 3 PM . "Oh my goodness, we've missed lunch!" he announced. He set out our food and then pulled out a large rabbit, tossing it into the air for Argil. Unfortunately for the rabbit, Argil swallowed it whole without chewing.

"After we eat, we'll start the preparations. We'll leave on Argil's back at 2 AM." As he stared into the empty space where Argil's voice had come from, Uncle Glorn asked Argil to try and rest before the crossing.

By 10 PM, I was dressed and ready. Uncle Glorn had done his best to explain how to assemble the Windsor knot. All our gear was packed, and for good measure, Uncle Glorn had laid out waterproof overalls for when we climbed out of the tent and back into the mud. I was puzzled by the fine clothes; it seemed strange given the people we'd encountered, and running in them was not ideal.

CHAPTER
8

I was supposed to be sleeping, but I lay there staring up at the ceiling. The tie felt worse than Argil's tail wrapped around my neck. The stiff jacket was itchy through my thin, clean collared shirt. Argil was fast asleep on my chest, his legs twitching in rhythm with the ticking of Uncle Glorn's watch. I was anxious, knowing all the hard work would be done by Argil.

"Please never leave me, Argil," I whispered. The edges of his lips curled up into a smile, but he continued to sleep, a small plume of steam rising with each breath. I focused on his warmth and drifted off to sleep.

I was once again pulled into my pocket world, but this time, I found myself seated on a throne. My parents appeared behind me, and the world I had created was just as I had left it during my first visit, minus the gleaming gold throne. I stood up and rushed into their arms. My mom spoke, "We have been watching you through the water pool you left for us in this place you created. We are no longer suspended in the darkness of Jeeves' pages." I focused, willing a small, furnished house into existence for them to relax in as they waited out the journey. "We need to confess something to you, but you cannot blame those responsible.' Before they could continue, I woke up to a soft licking sensation from Argil . I guess it wasn't the right time to learn their message.

I was curious about what they had to say, but since I couldn't control my access to this world, I decided to put it out of my mind. Today had enough trouble of its own. I was just glad they were in a physical, simulated world rather than in the darkness they had endured before. Argil interrupted my train of thought speaking in magic tongue, "It's time to leave, friend." I slowly sat up and looked around for Uncle Glorn, but he was gone. Near my wetsuit was a note:

Dear Jamez,

I am sorry I had to leave you like this. The arrangements for a safe journey with the Furtongues are meant for a young political leader's son. You will find your new idents in the pile. I leave you with Jeeves, my pouch, the tent, and all its contents. I love you, Jamez! You and Argil are more than capable of continuing the journey. I hope to see you again soon.

Love,
Uncle Glorn

Reading the letter left me winded. How could he leave? My parents were taken, even if not gone forever. I felt the weight of the loss hit me all at once. I was on my own.

Jeeves announced, "Not completely alone, Sir Levwick. Your parents would like to relay a message." A ball of light rose from the table and projected a video-like message. My dad spoke, "Son, I want you to focus. We don't understand why Glorn left, and it's crucial to avoid anger until the whole story is revealed. I know a huge burden is now on your shoulders. You are our hope for survival—not just for us, but for the next generation of Levwicks. We regret that you've been thrust into challenges that even adults would struggle with. This is temporary, and you will be the best of us through all your trials. You possess magic we never had at your age—let it guide you. Stay strong, use the map, and Jeeves will lead if needed. No matter the outcome, understand that we love you. Come visit us in your next dream."

The message lifted my heartache a bit. I felt the responsibility and burden emboldening me. As I walked toward Jeeves and the rest of the supplies, I reached to pick up the book, but at that moment, Jeeves and all the supplies levitated. I looked to my left, and the supplies revolved around me. It was strange; I hadn't used any magic to levitate the objects—they seemed to respond to my will. Jeeves called out, "Please stop showing off, sir; you're ruffling my pages." I slowed the rotation and gathered everything into the pouch. Perhaps this was how Uncle Glorn moved things around during our trip.

Argil, still on the bed, watched with wide eyes. If his jaw could have hit the floor, it would have. "Friend, I'm ready. Let's meet these furry-mouthed people," he voiced with a snuffling laugh.

We climbed the ladder as before, and as we exited, the tent's internals retracted. When I reached the top of the ladder, I cautiously peeked out, facing the sky. The moon was out, and everything was still. The sky moved rapidly, with clouds racing past the moon. I looked out over the desolate dirt landscape between the two fortifications. It resembled row after row of unwinding wire, like a massive thorn bush extending to my left and right.

What I hadn't realized before landing here was that we were outside NEDU's defenses, meaning Argil needed to travel through two fortified barriers. I spoke in magic tongue to Argil, careful not to alert anyone in the moonlit, battle-torn landscape. "Are you ready to go, Argil?"

Argil nodded "I'm ready," he said performing twisting and writhing stretches. At one point, he rotated his head 720 degrees. This dragon was truly strange and amazing—

enthralling and weird. I loved everything about Argil. Once he nodded in agreement, I moved all the remaining gear into the pouch, then pulled the pouch up to my waist and secured the drawstring around Argil's neck.

Like getting into a warm sleeping bag, I pulled the pouch up over my chest and then over my head into complete darkness. The sensation of being consumed by the pouch was entirely new, something my eyes and brain struggled to rationalize. It felt like my body was going numb, and I experienced no sensation of weight as I entered the weightless void of the bag.

Inside the pouch, I floated in darkness with only my thoughts and no sounds. The space didn't press in on me, as Uncle Glorn had worried—it was not painful or physically uncomfortable. Emotionally, it was a bit unnerving not knowing when I would be free. I hoped this wasn't how Mom and Dad experienced their limbo. No magic worked for me in the void—very handy as a prison, I pondered. I wondered if my uncle had created this pouch.

With no other means to pass the time, I formed inner dialogues and pondered how long I had been inside the void, hoping that time wasn't accelerated. The last thing I wanted was to exit as a 40-year-old man with the emotional IQ of an 11-year-old boy. My despairing thoughts eventually ran their course, and I drifted off to sleep.

Luckily, my dreams continued, but no matter how hard I tried, I couldn't reach out to my parents. I was left to my imagination. When I woke, I found myself in a bush as the sun was rising. Thank goodness I was back in the real world, though I had a very real burning sensation around my leg. Upon inspection, I discovered raw skin, scuffs, and scratches—likely from Argil pulling me out.

The pouch was still around Argil's neck. He looked exhausted and was fast asleep. I spoke to Jeeves in magic tongue, "What's next?"

"We are at the meeting point, but the Furtongues have not yet arrived, sir. Set up the tent and get into cover. I will alert you both when the guide arrives."

I freed the pouch from Argil and set up the tent and camouflage covering. I then carried Argil carefully inside and tucked him gently into the cot. "My little hero", I whispered. If only I could see what he had experienced during the crossing. Argil was in good health, with no scratches. Relief and happiness filled my heart. I cried, wishing Uncle Glorn could have been here to share this victory over the dangerous DMZ, all thanks to Argil. Who knows what would have happened without him?

"Jeeves," I called out loudly.

"Yes, Sir?" Jeeves replied.

I interrupted, "Please stop using such formal terms. Call me Jamez or Jame."

"Oh yes, si—Jame," Jeeves responded, his voice carrying an uncomfortable tone. "Any news?"

"None, si—my apologies, Jame. Calling any of you Levwicks by your first name denotes equality."

I interjected, "Jeeves, you're my friend, and I want us to be on a first-name basis."

"Okay, Jame, I'll attempt the requested changes."

I asked, "Where is my guide? It's nearly lunch. I thought they would have arrived by now. Are we not at the rendezvous location?"

"Yes we are at the right location, Jame, unfortunately, I have no more idea where they are than you do."

I sat down at the table and asked, "Is there anything we can do to pass the time?"

"I could resume your training, Jame."

"Not today, Jeeves. I'm going stir-crazy and having a hard time not pacing. I'm waiting and watching for any sight or sound."

"Perhaps turn on the comms and listen for a transmission," Jeeves suggested. I did as he recommended and turned up the volume. Static reverberated through the domed room, and a bad feeling came over me. How long had I been in the pouch?

I gently hugged Argil. He rolled over and looked up at me with a sad expression. "I'm sorry, Jamez. It took me three days to cross the DMZ. There were men in the trenches, and I hid until the loud sounds stopped. Forgive me," Argil repented with tears welling up in his eyes.

"It's okay, Argil. We're here now, and you did well," reassuring him as I patted his head. His face brightened, not quite smiling, but looking a great deal better. "We're alive and safe. Jeeves will help us get back on track."

The radio interrupted our solemn exchange with a man speaking in partial code. "Safe delivery and fur travel delayed due to border conflict escalation. Delayed another day. Meet by riverside bridge 1 mile west. Book knows alternate picnic spot. Wear jogging clothes; the ball was canceled."

I responded, "Copy, roger wilco," trying to mimic what I had heard my uncle say.

Jeeves explained, though I understood the basics: they were delayed, the new location was known only to Jeeves, and we needed to change out of our dress clothes. "I suggest we travel at night," Jeeves instructed. "My information on RONT is out of date."

CHAPTER
9

Argil and I had our meal. I was very impressed with how well Uncle Glorn had stocked his tent—there were emergency rations in every nook and cranny. Every drawer and cupboard was laid out and numbered in reverse order: 2028 days of food for a large family. I had been eating the meal from day 2028 for my last five meals and was only halfway through. Nothing was overly tasty but practical and healthy, and I was completely satiated after eating.

The day dragged on with little conversation and extra helpings of pacing the floor. For the first time, I heard Jeeves hum a tune as if he were reading a newspaper and relaxing.

"I don't mean to interrupt, Jeeves, but what song are you humming?" I asked.

He snapped, "Nothing, I didn't notice I was humming outloud."

As I cleaned up and put away all the supplies while sitting at the table I clumsily moved objects with my newly learned magic. Doing this required more concentration and effort than moving items by hand. Each item I moved required more strain, and after a short break, I could move the supplies more easily. It was amusing to feel out the limits of my new magical abilities, so I spent time moving and rearranging items, testing the limits of "object push."

"Ahem," Jeeves interrupted my exercise. "We need to

be moving along to the next location."

I put down the books and papers I was juggling and pulled Jeeves from across the room. "Open to page 250," Jeeves expressed with irritation in his voice.

I opened Jeeves to page 250 and saw the path we needed to take. The map was topographical, and the route he plotted, marked in red ink, climbed across the page over the waving lines. "Does this mean elevation?" I asked, pointing to a spot midway between the start and end of the red line.

"That denotes a steep part of the rock," Jeeves explained. "It will be challenging, but we must avoid this valley road and the checkpoint here." A blue line appeared, indicating a more direct route. "The orange circle is the vicinity of the checkpoint."

"We don't want to be anywhere near the road while RONT is recovering from a combat event at the border." Everything was packed—myself, Argil, and Jeeves, like the three amigos. From a distance, it would look like a lost child talking to himself and carrying an invisible pet. Everything was moved into the pouch. Outside the tent it was quiet, a nice, cool breeze pressed my t-shirt and light shorts against my chilled skin. The moon was full, casting its light across the landscape. My eyes adjusted to the low light, and a visual image of our progress across the map projected into my imagination, thanks to Jeeves sending details via magic tongue.

The mountain rock face jutted up in front of me, and we scaled it for a few hours until it became too steep to climb higher. Still following the moving marker in my head, we navigated the sprawling landscape around the mountain rocks. When we reached the other side, I could see the train bridge in the distance, partly obscured by the treetops. Climbing down was my favorite part; I was now carrying a sleeping Argil.

I arrived at the old iron train drawbridge which was over a wide river. Jeeves finally notified me that we had arrived. Moments after, three hooded figures emerged from the bushes their faces obscured by a magical covering. "Quickly, Jamez," Jeeves urged. There was no time for introductions; not a word was spoken as I was helped onto the back of a giant elk. I hoped these were the Furtongue guides, though I wondered who else would randomly offer transportation.

We started to gallop down the valley. I opened my mouth to yell a greeting to the hooded people riding alongside me, but I felt a force push my jaw back closed. One of the hooded figures, mid-ride, had silenced me with a raised hand. They placed their index finger to their lips, signaling to be quiet. I had forgotten about the magic tongue for some odd reason.

I heard the lady's voice in my head: "No noise, no questions. We are being tracked by a drone. They cannot know who is riding these elk" I nodded, watching the lady to my right. Her riding style was mesmerizing; her entire body seemed to float above the elk. The elk was bumping and moving, but unlike my paint shaker ride, she was half-standing, her legs absorbing the jostling while her upper body remained still and stable.

I could hear the buzzing of the drone, and then a loud voice projected from it: "Stop and submit for ident." After the message played on repeat, the lady who had quieted me earlier grabbed the reins of my elk, and we veered to the left. The other two riders slowed to a stop with the drone overhead. It was difficult to gauge the drone's size until it landed beside the giant elk. Compared to the two people, the drone was as big as a pickup truck. As it descended, its shape became visible: four turbine-like structures arranged where the wings of a dragonfly would be, and two machine guns mounted on an underslung turret.

We rode away until the repeating message became a mere whisper. We traveled west for three miles before stopping to give the elk a break. The lady pulled back her cloak hood her facial features still obscured by the magic veil and introduced herself. "I am Lady Terra of the Furtungues, kindred to your family, the Levwicks." She bowed to me. "Your Majesty, I am at your service."

My mind recalled Uncle Glorn's note, explaining that my cover idents were those of a political leader's son. At that moment, I had no idea if this was a clever ruse by Uncle Glorn or if this was simply how politicians were treated in RONT. Either way, I wasn't going to dissuade her, as I didn't want to offend her by rejecting her customary greeting. She approached me, "My Lord, forgive me for silencing you earlier; you were in danger." She helped me off the elk and then lowered back into a bow. I changed my mind, smiling at her display and mannerisms, which mirrored Jeeves when I first met him.

"Everything is OK, and please call me by my first name, Jamez." I wasn't going to spend this long trip listening to inefficient royal platitudes. "Please save the formalities for when the surroundings require it, but one-on-one, my friends call me Jame."

She returned to standing upright with an astonished expression. "What now?" I asked, eager to change the subject. Lady Terra was so committed to my cover story that it was painful to watch.

"Well, Jame," her voice trembling as she said my name for the first time, "we need to switch to a new animal since the drones will come in greater numbers now, and it needs to be a more stealthy one."

Two full-grown dragons flickered into view, tied to a post, and then disappeared again. My goodness, I thought—grown gypsy dragons! As I grasped where Argil was, and whispered in magic tongue, "Do you see them?" He shook and replied in magic tongue, "Yes." I was confused by his fear, as they could be distant relatives of his.

Lady Terra continued, "These are invisible gypsy dragons." She looked at me, waiting for a reaction—perhaps a gasp or shock. She didn't wait long. "Their wings, when overlapped around you, can conceal you from all earthly tracking systems." Except common mud, I scoffed to myself, and held back a chuckle. "We must be on our way now, my... eh, Jame."

We approached the dragons, which were visible to me without the amulet. Argil could remain invisible at all times without the amulet in my hand—strange. Lady Terra might have spent less time if she had known I had a baby talking gypsy dragon. Argil snarled in magic tongue, "The Furtongues remove the dragons' voices during domestication, so don't expect them to talk. Brutes." Argil snorted, luckily without being heard. "Argil has memory of this but nothing else."

After Argil shared that, my opinion of the Furtongues soured a bit, but I was grateful for the heads-up
"Jeeves," I asked in magic tongue, "is this true?"

"Sadly, yes, Jame however the silencing of the dragons is more complicated than just stopping them from speaking at all times. I need you to learn the block spell. When she falls asleep, I will teach you."

CHAPTER 10

I climbed onto the dragon, which was devoid of any expression. I felt a pang of sadness for them; they were magnificent and large dragons. The dragons took on a slow, clumsy walk, swaying back and forth with a rolling movement down their backs as their hind legs moved with each step. I was sure this was going to be a long trip. Although the dragons appeared to walk slowly, their strides were long and they were faster than I could run at full speed. They weren't as fast as the elk, but the trade-off for invisibility and consistent speed with little strain on the animals meant we could travel like this for many hours between rests. According to Lady Terra, we could travel at least eight hours at a time.

I wondered to myself why we weren't flying. Jeeves, hearing my thought, ran into a brief explanation. "They can fly for longer distances, but at the cost of their invisibility. All the wild gypsy dragons seem to choose a passive existence on the ground. Being this large in a world full of unnatural predators and fearful humans is a risk they tend to avoid. When they do fly, it's for short distances to escape imminent threats. These dragons we ride are reserved for very selective circumstances."

"Fascinating," I replied to Jeeves, and I wasn't even being sarcastic. It was very interesting how much Jeeves really did know. The statement from my uncle drifted through my head: "He will share information at the time it is needed."

As much as possible, Lady Terra led us down abandoned roads and through dense forests. The dragons moved like a snakes whisper; Jeeves told me they had a sensory awareness of their entire close environment, like sonar, allowing them to navigate even without vision. I experienced this firsthand as we moved through the thick woods. Their bodies bent and slinked as if they had no bones or spine, which made me dizzy from the chaotic movements at a consistent speed. I fell asleep several times before we reached the first stable safe house.

I secretly set up the tent while Lady Terra prepared the location for visitors, pulling sheets of camouflage fabric away to allow the dragons to get under cover. As the first day drew to a close, I waited for Lady Terra to fall asleep and took in the picturesque pine trees surrounding the log stable. Our hammocks were set up in the loft, with several magical alarm charms at the doors and paths leading to the open-air stable. The stable had a green metal roof with a splattering of rust, resembling a Jackson Pollock painting from ten feet away. The outside was shaded by pine trees, casting shadows day and night.

By 2 a.m., I finally heard the rhythmic air passing through Lady Terra's sinuses, producing an annoying whistling noise—another endearing quirk of hers. Part of me hoped these quirks would grow on me. Sneaking past her hammock, I avoided stepping on the creaking steps by straddling the banister and inching my way down to the ground level, carefully avoiding all the magical traps that shone bright with the amulet but were invisible without it.

I always had Argil, the pouch, and Jeeves with me, inside or outside of the pouch; it didn't matter. Jeeves, annoyingly able to read my thoughts, asked, "What's that, Jame?" I successfully tuned out 90% of this banter. Jeeves

CH-PG 10-56

raised his voice as if protesting, "Shut up, Jamez, you don't even know what I'm about to say."

"Well, I imagine you have a point to make," I replied.

"Well, thanks to you and your incessant inner dialog, you made me forget." It was strange; somehow, our connection seemed to be growing stronger. I raised my voice, yelling in magic tongue to argue back, "LEAVE MY THOUGHTS ALONE!" The blast of magic tongue woke Lady Terra, who noticed my empty hammock and sprinted to the lower level in search of me.

I jumped into the tent, and Argil laid on top of the flap, making the entrance invisible to Lady Terra. Now, I needed to come up with an excuse for my disappearance. Jeeves began urgently, "We have a minute. This is not ideal. The block and push spells are very similar—imagine the push spell collapsing into itself," he explained quickly. "The shape code is a shovel shape. The faster it flashes in your vision, the stronger the block is. But be warned, it can be very taxing on your magic with strong blocks and attacks."

I created a block while pulling a can of soup through the air toward my head like a speeding bullet. The shield flashed, and the can exploded on contact.

"That concludes—" Before he could finish, I was out of the tent, collecting the items and tucking them away. As I turned, Lady Terra grabbed me and barked, "Explain yourself, my liege." Her voice was stern, and her eyes scolded me. I snapped, "I have stomach cramps and needed privacy." Her expression turned neutral, and she softly relayed the protocol: moving forward, I would need to wake her and be accompanied.

I felt like a little kid, but she was right. She wasn't concerned with my loud magic tongue message; she fervently wanted to protect me. While this didn't change my distrust of her, it did erode my emotional barrier just a tiny bit. I protested the fleeting idea of investing trust in Lady Terra. She escorted me back to my hammock and then stayed upright at the highest side, her unblinking eyes fixed in my direction.

"Jeeves?" I asked.

"Yes, Jame," he replied.

"I don't think I'll be able to pull that little stunt again."

"Yes, I have to concur. I will work lessons in as we travel."

Despite the broken sleep, I woke up feeling rested and strong. Looking around, I noticed I was missing my amulet. As I looked down, I saw my hands were also glowing. "I found it, Jamez, it's in the tent," I called out, sensing it there. The amulet then phased into existence in my hand as I pulled it from an expansion void.

"You need to put that back on or you may lose control of your magic again," Jeeves stated. I hesitated; the surge of energy radiated both internally and visually around me. I brought the pendant to my head, and an opaque, foggy mirror appeared before me. My eyes locked with red eyes glowing from under the hood of a cloaked man sitting on a throne made entirely of human and magical creature bones. A booming voice projected into my head: "I WILL FIND YOU, JAMEZ."

This was overwhelming, and I broke out of my unblinking trance, quickly placing the amulet around my neck. "The viewing portal is closed, Jamez," Jeeves stated. "You mustn't be so careless in the future."

"Who was that?" I shot back at Jeeves.

"I was in your head and saw what you witnessed. He may be the hidden power controlling the magi. I have searched my memory and have no recollection of his voice nor the throne's whereabouts."

I gained a newfound respect for the relic Uncle Glorn

had given me and its function. Like an infomercial, it played out in my head: "It protects, it stores, it hides, slices, and dices—all this and more for 4 easy payments of never EVER removing the amulet again." I also discovered I had two new abilities I had no control over. The first of which was the ability to pull an item to me from another place only by sensing it. The second ability which I hope to never accidentally use again was opening up a communication window. Before this, I would forget I was wearing the amulet; now, I felt for it at every waking and sleeping moment. The sensation of magic was intoxicating and called to me, but my fear of the hooded evil figure dissuaded my impulse to indulge.

Fortunately, Lady Terra was out of earshot of this mornings call from evil anonymous. I wouldn't have known how to begin to explain what had happened if she had responded to the commotion. As I wandered out of the stable I noticed Lady Terra out near the pines tending to the dragons—feeding, washing, and brushing them. I couldn't help but imagine a mundane watching her feed thin air and scrub thin air. This notion amused Jeeves, and I heard him laugh for the first time. He was becoming more animated with each passing day—more human, with more moods and less like a computer. I felt strongly that my connection with him was influencing him. I wasn't sure if it was bad or good, but one thing was obvious: neither of us knew how to separate the bindings.

I also enjoyed the effortless communication and real-time input as things occurred. I didn't want him out of my head after all. Jeeves interjected, "I must admit it is normalizing for me." I agreed with my internal dialogue. Lady Terra called from outside, "It's time to saddle up and be on our way." For some reason, it vaguely reminded me of the old Westerns my dad used to watch at Fort Patience. I climbed into the saddle, refusing Lady Terra's objections and her attempts to help.

The dragon's wings closed over me, leaving a small viewing hole no bigger than my head. Argil was snuggled into my lap, getting much-needed scritches, while Jeeves was safely inside the pouch, sporadically announcing things he had never personally seen as we traveled.

CHAPTER
11

We stealthily passed another Slyherder, accidentally bumping his cowboy hat off. I thought, these guys sure have a thing for over-the-top fashion statements. It's not enough that they're riding a growing plant. What happens if they forget something at home? I amused both myself and Jeeves with wacky observations and obvious questions. It felt like having a carefree family renting space in my head, talking and joking with Argil, Jeeves, and myself. This was how we passed the time during the trip.

Nothing of note happened for a solid week. Lady Terra followed the same routine every day, and I adhered to all her rules, as awkward as some of them were. The fear of the man with red eyes gradually moved farther out of my mind, but the lesson would never leave me. As we traveled, Argil helped himself to the pouch's near-endless supply of "Argil food," as he called it. His tail was perpetually inside the pouch, pulling out animals like a sadistic magician, making the same surprised and elated look each time another random rodent popped out.

I am now fully convinced that the pouch either had a severe infestation of small animals or Uncle Glorn spent months collecting them. Both options seemed too amazing to rule out. Maybe it's both, I laughed out loud. Were there hundreds or thousands of them just floating in the pouch's void, living out their existence as if this were normal, unaware of anything different? Little milk cartons with "Missing Ratty" on the label danced through my mind. I was aware my imagination was not just wandering but that it had ventured into an entirely different galaxy.

After 30 days, we had traveled through Tennessee and entered Mississippi without any problems or hiccups. The route was a major magical route, much like the old Underground Railroad I learned about in school. The route had regular rest points, perfectly spaced at 8-hour intervals.

My new chief concern was Argil. He was growing rapidly and was no longer able to travel on my lap; he was now the size of a small pony. He followed behind the larger dragons, and I feared I would soon be unable to hide him. His appetite now outpaced the pouch rations, and he spent our rest stops hunting larger animals. He had developed a fondness for what he called masked bears commonly known as raccoons. These weren't like the raccoons of Earth from Uncle Glorn's early life. These creatures were 5 feet tall, as dangerous as the old world bears, and highly intelligent. They also hunted humans in large family groups. Luckily, their large size made them slow, clumsy, and loud. You could hear them lumbering through the forest from nearly 1,000 feet away. I had heard their voices; they hated being so big and complained the whole time—a chorus of 30 members commiserating almost in unison as I listened from the safety of the dragons.

Along with his increased size, Argil's intelligence and vocabulary were now four times more advanced. Jeeves had no information to add about the growth speed; all we seemed to know came from the dragons we were riding. He was certainly going to become a big boy.

On day 31, during our ride at noon, I hit a bump, and the amulet bounced into the air. It was only out of contact briefly when a lock appeared in my vision. The lock hovered over the dragon and then disappeared from view as the amulet fell back against my chest. Jeeves commented before I could say anything, "Jame, that is the lock preventing their voice."

This notion resurfaced my disgust for the Furtongues. I was determined to unlock it. I had no idea how and was strongly afraid of seeing the red-eyed lord if I removed the amulet to attempt to pick the voice lock on my dragon. "The repercussions could affect relations between families," Jeeves added. "I strongly advise you leave it alone."

I devised a plan, albeit one that I regretted as Jeeves countered each step. "It's not really a plan, Jeeves. I get it. I was going to have Argil hold the amulet away from my body while I picked the lock. If anything else occurred, like another visit from the big boogie man, Argil would drop it onto my neck, ending the experiment. What could possibly go wrong?"

Jeeves started listing every conceivable outcome, the chief of which was breaking the lock, freeing the animal's voice permanently, and damaging the trust between families. During this attempt, I didn't need to leave my hammock, but Lady Terra still needed to be asleep; otherwise, she might see the lock being picked and interrupt, ruining my chance of ever unlocking this mystery.

I decided this time I would have Argil wake me after Lady Terra slept. Jeeves, in my head, begrudgingly agreed to help if needed. Around 3 AM, Argil was calling to me in magic tongue, nudging me with his body, his head leaning over my face. He was almost too big to be in this space, but his contorted and twisted body allowed him to sneak up to the loft without issue. We got into position; Argil was all set, grasping the chain of the amulet.

I felt around the area with my magic sensitivity,

focused in the direction of the dragons. They were lying in piles of hay just below us. I locked onto the sensation of the dragons. "Now, Argil," I whispered in magic tongue. He lifted the pendant, and immediately the lock appeared. It was the same style as Jeeves' but was made for Furtongue's magic. Wait, I was part Furtongue, I pondered. Couldn't hurt to try. Jeeves was waiting; I could feel him focus on this moment, but he kept silent.

The lock was six stacked diamonds. I closed my eyes and sensed the first latch position. I turned the lock, and the first star fell to the ground in front of me like a fire spark, falling to the ground and turning from an amber flame into white ash. I continued this five more times. At the last star, a flash of light wrapped around the corners of the house and up the wall to where I was, like the lights cast into your house from a passing vehicle at night, only much brighter, originating from the dragon.

Immediately, the dragon spoke to me, soft and regal, with an ancient weight in his voice. "Jamez, you are not safe here or with Lady Terra. She is unaware that she is leading you to the Lord of the Magi, where you would be in great danger." The magic lock started glowing and regenerating. The last words I barely made out were, "Tell my son, Argileous, I love him. I am sorry I sent him away for his saf..." The lock recovered, cutting off the dragon mid-sentence.

As this happened, Argil dropped the amulet in horror at the news. "Mom and Dad!" he exclaimed with a shaking voice, "they spoke over me and revealed my lost memory." Argil freely shared the flood of memories in magic tongue, the following memories hit me all at once:

"I woke up inside a golden sphere, hearing muffled voices—one high-pitched, the other low and deep. The voices drew closer, and the sphere rolled onto its side, pressing my legs against my face. Sensations pulsed through my newly perceived limbs, tail, and wings. This was my awakening, and though everything felt strange, I knew things I hadn't been taught. I was a dragon, and my parents were nearby, providing warmth. A human voice, speaking our language with an accent, approached my glowing gold home.

'How is he?' a woman's voice reverberated through my sphere, followed by my fathers deep, heavy voice, thick with concern: 'Our son has awoken, but he's seven days late.'

'Oh my,' the woman replied. I would later find out this was Lady Terra.

'What should we do?' Terra asked.

'There's nothing to be done. It is up to Argilious now.'

I caught a glimpse of our birthplace, an island filled with lotus flowers. I knew it was where we were made, though I had never been there. The island was hardwired into me. A chill ran down my spine, and instinctively, my wings expanded, forcing the hooked tips to break through my confines. I rolled out onto a straw bed as Lady Terra exclaimed, 'An empty shell?'

'No, he's refusing to be seen. This is normal; he's new to the world,' my father explained.

I clumsily rolled away from the egg and back into the warmth of my mother's tail. Lady Terra, although unable to see me, looked relieved. She stood up after straining to catch a glimpse of me in vain, 'Well, I'll return tomorrow for your grooming.'

After Lady Terra left the stable, I felt her presence grow distant. I remembered my parents arguing about me.

'We need to free him from this indentured servitude,' my father grieved. He didn't want me to live the same life he and my mother had. 'For Argilious to be made as a gift to Terra's offspring is a lowly existence.'

My mother agreed. 'When you can hunt on your own, we will set you free.' This was about a month later, as I recall.

I learned to shift my scales from invisible to visible. According to my parents, I was an anomaly. I possessed stronger wing muscles and lighter bone density. My father explained, 'Your refractive scales are perfectly formed, with no birth or familial defects. This allows you to be completely invisible, even to a powerful wizard like Lady Terra. No level of magic can expose you; only by your choice can you be seen. For 99.999% of our ancestors, advanced magic could force them to be visible. If not for this, our existence would still remain hidden from magical humans. You are the rarest dragon in Earth's history, and that is why you must go. Your value as a weapon far exceeds your destiny as a gift to Terra's child.'"

Snapping back from the vision, Argil announced with authority, "We need to run." Jeeves reluctantly agreed, saying, "We have no idea how far-reaching the attempts on your life have influenced RONT and the honorable Furtongue family. As much as it pains me, I agree." My belongings were still packed. Argil suggested I hide in the pouch again while we fled in a random direction.

CHAPTER 12

While I was relaxing in the mouse void pouch, I was planning a new route to avoid the old one and the Magi. The old route we were using was no longer safe, knowing the evil could be anywhere along the way. Next thing I knew, a hand reached into the pouch and pulled me out by the ear. I had no idea how long I was inside the pouch, but Lady Terra was dirty, her hair flat and salted with dust. She looked a mess. Argil was breathing heavily and visibly covered in dirt. Her face was not upset but concerned. I would understand why she would have been angry; this effect on a person does not happen without a large passing of time.

She grabbed my collar and my arm, helping me up. "I need to explain some things to you, and I didn't spend three days chasing your dragon without an explanation," insisted Lady Terra. I was choked up but shared what the male dragon had conveyed. "Let me stop you there. That was true. The other two riders were working for the Magi. Those traitors, when discovered, were taken into custody on that day. The dragon only knew half of the mission and alerted me to the danger. These dragons are locked from talking to anyone not inside our inner circle of trusted family members. We are heading away from, not towards, a trap. The only sin I am guilty of is not sharing more information. The leader is too powerful to take on directly, so my troop has—or was—

leading Cedar of the Kaos family away, and very successfully, until you opened an instant comms portal to him. I am unsure how you performed this ancient and deadly magic, and I don't care. Your dragon is okay, just very exhausted. These dragons are in service to their king, and what sentient being would enjoy being forced to remain quiet?"

The three of us traveled for three days before we found the next safe stable. According to Lady Terra, we had a sufficient lead on the Magi forces who were in pursuit. We rested, and the dragons collapsed upon entering the stable. This detour I created in Lady Terra's planned schedule stressed the dragons to their limits. The added weight of Argil slung over the back of my dragon had not helped the stress and strain of our three days without rest. Though the dragons did not speak, they did have subtle ways of communicating that I started to pick up on. At this moment they appeared frustrated, understandable given what they had just gone through.

On our first rest after I had run off, I fell into such a deep sleep and Uncle Glorn weighed heavy at the front of my mind. I would do anything just to know he was okay. Why did he run away? As I drifted off to sleep, I saw 200 flashing shapes circling around a tunnel. I was falling through what looked like a wormhole. The swirling center changed into a pixelated live feed, then came into focus. I was back in the tent, looking down at a letter. Only this letter was the one Uncle Glorn had written.

I was watching Uncle Glorn write the short, vague message. I could see the world through his eyes and hear his thoughts. Was this his memory? Was I in the past, watching and learning? Why and how could any of this be real? One thing I was sure about: this was not an average dream, and I hoped I could get enough answers to my burning questions before I woke up. I strained to look around, but nothing moved. I tried to talk to Uncle Glorn, but nothing came out. I was a passenger on this trip and had no control. I now felt off about knowing his internal contemplations, fearing what I might learn could break my high esteem of this man who was a superhero to me. Even if I wanted to, I didn't know how to control my time watching, either to extend my viewing time or end it. I shut off my brain and decided not to struggle against it in any way, positive or negative. "Just a passenger," I repeated to myself.

Uncle Glorn got up, double, then triple-checked the room, looked over the food, and emptied three large sacks full of various rodents and small animals into his pouch. I will regret this, he mused. Uncle Glorn collected all the supplies and placed them on the table with the letter on top. He walked over to Argil's imprint on the bed and woke him up. "Take care of him, Argil." He was invisible, but I could hear him yawn. "I hope I get to see you again, Argil. Please wait until I leave to wake up Jamez. I go to prepare his path through RONT in advance". However the mystery of who was breaking into Cubby Hold Garden was also on his mind. As Uncle Glorn prepared to leave the tent he began sobbing—a strong giant but soft as a teddy bear, I reflected. Climbing the steps, he returned to his solemn state of mind, a man on a mission.

His thoughts shifted gears abruptly, and he was sprinting away from the DMZ. NEDU started trailing him with a hail of bullets from every direction, like tens of hundreds of metal roofs being pounded by hail. He stopped and formed a blue shield. The wall filled with lead, frozen in the barrier. A flash, then the entire exchange slowed down to 1/100th of normal speed. He was typing in his vision, a sentence of magical shapes. Even with him slowing time around him, I could barely follow the magic. There was no chance of memorizing this. I was exhilarated to witness a master at work. At the end of the spell, he extracted the kinetic energy from the lead frozen in front of him. He redirected the absorbed energy at every muzzle flash. In every direction, people were thrown into the air and frozen unconscious. Glorn took great effort to stun, injure, and render the soldiers unconscious but not kill a single one. Everything was slowed down in his magic area of influence. He casually walked past them all, still hanging in the air, then falling as they were out of his range. They were all asleep when he walked out of the area. Looking back, he remarked, "These men know not what they do." But he had a sort of love for them despite their efforts to destroy him. So much control and care were taken in that instance that it would have been easy for Uncle Glorn not to show restraint. He clearly was on a whole other level of power. "Murder is wrong, and I will not be like these monsters." At that last statement, I was pulled back, and again the wormhole was in front of me as I fell backward.

CH-PG 12-70

I landed hard enough in the hammock that one of the anchors ripped out of the wood post it was attached to. This was not a dream, I concluded, as I landed back here with a crash. I was so happy I wasn't even disappointed with the very brief view of Uncle Glorn's exit and subsequent battle. I was impressed and envisioned, this is how I want to be when I grow up. He was even-tempered, logical, tender with strong morals, taking on challenging and dangerous tasks. I needed to get moving for the morning. Argil was rested and back to his goofy self, prancing through the forest, only visible when he bounced above the low bushes. He hunted in the most hilarious way, and as morbid as this may be, the critters were eaten with exclamations of surprise. They didn't get a chance to fear, it was a humane ending for the animals and, to quote Argil, "a dragon's gotta eat."

CHAPTER 13

The weather was slowly getting colder each day. Lady Terra was performing her chores as if nothing had gone horribly awry for six days straight. She chased me down like a lost sheep and still held no bitterness against me. I was very lucky to be in her care. We saddled up, and Jeeves prepared my lesson for the next eight hours. Jeeves started with, "Okay, everyone, class is in session. Please take your seats. Jamez, put down your phone and pay attention." If this was a joke, I didn't get it and asked, "What is a phone?" Jeeves sighed, "Never mind, Jamez. We will cover the seven other families, starting with a high-level overview. Three families focused on industry, weapons, and energy or electricity. The other four focused on social function, medicine for mundanes, law and policing, and finance and banking. The three families— Koal with a K, Aslocks, and Surlings—joined to form Kaos. The next four families—Dockternals, Justinds, Goldens, and Accountsinants—possessed residual magic that made them an exceptionally fortunate group. They excelled in success but gave up wielding magic. Over time, they intermarried with mundanes and multiplied their offspring with little regard to magic until magic was nearly nonexistent. Today, no official house remains under any of these names."

Traveling through Mississippi was no easy task when our objective was to avoid major roads and populated areas.

Luckily, there were no high-traffic areas in our path. Eight hours had passed relatively quickly, but we were nowhere near the next stable on the route. The terrain was swampy, the sky was hazy, and it was raining heavily—so heavily that Lady Terra used a rain-repelling spell for the first time on our trip. We stopped abruptly on a small hill jutting out of the mud and green water.

"We will set up camp here for the night," Lady Terra announced, disappointment heavy in her voice. We were under the canopy of three twisting trees that looked like a large wave in a "C" shape. I offered to set up my—or should I say Uncle Glorn's—tent. Lady Terra replied, "No need." This was the first time I was close enough to see her wield magic.

She had a casting ring on each hand. The left-hand ring looked like a coiled snake with its mouth open over her knuckle as if it were actively biting, its eyes two large cushion-cut diamonds. The right-hand casting ring looked like a large wedding band. She raised her hands facing the tangled tree trunks, spoke a magic phrase, and white, warm light emanated from the stones. The vines creaked and groaned in defiance but obeyed the instruction. They rolled and contorted into a lean-to, then the walls formed, and finally, grass grew rapidly from the ground and turned to straw. With a swift hand movement, she threshed the grass and stacked it into neatly packed beds for our dragons. Our hammocks looked like inchworms, inching and climbing into the tree limbs. Lady Terra pulled down on her vest.

I watched her magic with great fascination. Until now, I had not "been in the kitchen watching the food be prepared," so to speak. The way she cast magic was very different from how Uncle Glorn and I could cast without instruments. Her form and method were impressive and in no way inferior to how the Levwicks used magic—just different and unique. Lady Terra interrupted my thoughts, "We need to rush off to sleep tonight, no dilly-dallying. We leave at 6 AM tomorrow."

Thank goodness, I said to myself, grateful we had nimble dragons jumping and weaving around the hills, dotting between the green pools of water. Traveling through the swamp was extremely laborious. The little fort she constructed was water- and windproof. The night in the swamp was anything but quiet—the symphony of creatures filled my head as I drifted off to sleep.

Just like the night before, I was greeted with the path to Uncle Glorn's mind. I was so happy to be back, but he was not where I had last seen him. This time he was back inside Cubby Hold Garden, the entire interior blackened from what Uncle Glorn believed was a massive explosion. Uncle Glorn was holding a reflection stone, watching the events that occurred after we left. A smoky, shiny afterimage was overlaid and playing at half speed, similar to when you stare at an object for a long time, then close your eyes and the image lingers in your vision.

A fireball could be seen breaking through the entrance, enveloping the courtyard and burning all the plants in an instant. The man I saw in the viewing mirror walked around inside the structure, realizing we had left the time-dilated room and that the same speed delay that allowed us to escape into KONT would also hold up the hooded man in the garden. He slammed his fist onto the round table in the center of the room, destroying it, and its parts flew in all directions. Then he exited.

The reflection Uncle Glorn was watching had no sound, but my imagination filled in the blanks. Uncle Glorn knew this man by name, "Cedar of Kaos." With that last statement, I was yanked back and found myself in the still of the morning, lying in the hammock. My uncle was investigating the assailant. I was fuzzy on the timeline, unsure where I was when he was at Cubby Hold Garden, and with the pocket world time dilation, it was hard to guess where he was and when I was at each moment. I was now very hopeful that I might see him again. Perhaps he passed Cedar's name onto Lady Terra somehow.

The sun was barely rising above the swamp, casting emerald green hues through the windows and onto my face. Frost formed at the edges of the room as the season shifted into warm yellows and browns—my favorite time of year. I got up to take in all the sounds and the fall décor. Lady Terra, still making that whistle-like snoring sound, to no surprise, had not grown on me. Falling asleep was always a race to avoid the sounds of Lady Terra's rest—a race I never won. She, unfortunately, possessed the ability to fall asleep within moments of her head hitting the netting of her hammock.

Jeeves interrupted my silence. As great as sharing my headspace with a nearly all-knowing book might have sounded, it was wearing on my nerves. The only positive part was that I couldn't hide this frustration. Jeeves continued, "I too feel this way, both of those sentiments."

"Easy for you," I replied. "I can't hear your inner dialogue, but you freely hear mine. Is it possible for you to knock before coming in?" I asked. Then I added, "Could you tune out my inner dialogues during my casual ponderings?"

"I will make the requested changes," his voice returning to the old Jeeves from when I first met him. I felt guilty, but my sanity was at stake.

Two days passed with no word from Jeeves and no tunneling into Uncle Glorn's mind. Our pace was returning to normal as we left the swamps and entered plains and old farmlands, now vacant of human life. Small towns looked as if life had stopped; people had abandoned their belongings, cars, and houses, allowing nature and a horror of unnatural animals to move in. Hearing all the animals' conversations was no help—a series of obvious statements and endless needs. I yearned for Gavlow's level of developed personality.

"Jeeves," I called.

"Yes, sir Levwick. How may I assist you?" he retorted with an uninterested tone.

"I see a connection between your involvement in my thoughts and the entering of Uncle Glorn's memory. Could you explain this?"

"Certainly, si—" I interrupted, "Call me Jame. I didn't want an all-or-nothing effect on our interactions. I just needed space inside my own head, but I can see this has hurt you, and for that, I'm sorry. This wasn't me rejecting you; I enjoy talking to you. Some internal observations don't need a reply unless circumstances require your intervention—safety, bad judgment, etc."

"Yes, J-Jame, I was hurt, and I have never experienced this range of emotions personally. I too hold blame. Seeing through your eyes and sharing your experiences has been the most exhilarating experience I've felt in my very long existence. In my own way, I am growing up, and these new and personal emotions are a very real challenge for me. I am sorry for relentlessly invading your mind."

"I forgive you, Jeeves. I'm only eleven, but don't hesitate to discuss these new emotions as they come up."

"To attempt an answer: the correlation between our connection and your ability to cast the mind tunneling—and really all the magic you've cast without difficulty—is becoming clear. I believe, as plain as the new hair above your lip, that you're pulling the spells from your ancestors through me. I am at a loss to explain how you accomplish this, but it seems the more magic you pull, the stronger our bond becomes. From what I've witnessed at each event, you have a strong emotional pull, and then you flawlessly carry out your intense desire. This is all very fascinating for me." Another of Uncle Glorn's sayings popped into my head:

"Nothing is free." It might not have perfectly fit the context, but every time I used magic with Jeeves, the barrier between us weakened. Little shifts, adding up quickly. Reflecting on all the magic I had performed, I realized I was unknowingly creating my own dilemma, and now I had no idea how to prevent it from advancing further. How could I discipline my wants and needs? I was an eleven-year-old being forced to grow up in an instant—or I could accept the unknown merging that would undoubtedly occur.

Making this decision was the only reasonable course of action. I would continue down this road because I couldn't accept restricting this astronomical magic advantage. Perhaps this ancient wizard could show me an alternative or a way to reverse the connection. It was a lot to decide. Without noticing the trip in front of me, we arrived at the next location, and I didn't even remember boarding the dragon or the eight-hour journey. I would choose Jeeves and the unknown.

I spoke to Jeeves, "Do you accept this decision as well? It could be permanent."

Jeeves replied without hesitation, "This experience has been the highlight of my entire existence, and I would be honored to travel this road with you. With understanding and mutual empathy, we could accomplish anything."

It was settled—we would continue to grow together, both of us prepared for the unpreparable, as per usual.

"What could go wrong?" Jeeves and I shared a short-lived laugh before I prepared my hammock for bed. I felt both the loss of experiencing normal life and the excitement of what would come with the family's magical knowledge. On second thought, I had no idea what I was missing, but I did understand what I was gaining.

I asked Jeeves, "Do you have a guestimate of how connected we'll become?"

"Well," he replied, "if it continues at this pace, we could end up finishing..."

"Each other's sentences!" I blurted out in a silly tone.

"Yes," he replied, with a tone that seemed to carry a smile within it. "It's impossible to know the extent of something that has never been known to occur in any of the ten families—and each family possesses a book like me."

Tucked comfortably into my hammock, I asked Jeeves, "Could we visit Uncle Glorn tonight?"

CHAPTER
14

This time, instead of tunneling into Uncle Glorn's memory, I found myself in a third-person perspective inside a laboratory. Discolored scrolls were on several rolling chalkboards, hastily drawn shapes covering every exposed black slate. Jeeves exclaimed, "Fascinating, isn't it?" I wasn't sure what I was witnessing.

I looked down from above at a man in a white lab coat. The tables and desks were cluttered with beakers, dirty dishes, old copper and bronze apparatuses, spoons, and pliers. As I scanned the room, I noticed the bottom half of a newspaper, with the publish date in bold Roman numerals and Italian writing. I couldn't read it, but luckily Jeeves could, and he spoke, "June 18th, 1932. Italy's Chronicles of the Mages for the Ages."

It was a magical illustrated newspaper. Jeeves continued, "This is the exact day dream tunneling was discovered. Among the mess sat an old man, his name was Tristian A. Levwick. He had long gray hair and thin, emaciated high cheekbones. He was frail, skin and bones, his clothing baggy, torn, and dirty, with soot all over his body. This man's appearance screamed dedication above all else. Hygiene and regular meals were clearly luxuries he could not afford. In his scrawny, pale hands was Jeeves' book."

Jeeves added, "I have no personal recollection of this

day—it was, of course, before my birth."

"Your birth?" I asked.

"I gained awareness in 1975, so I consider that my birthdate," Jeeves explained.

Tristan lurched up, startling me, and my attention fixed on him as he darted over to the chalkboard and changed the recipe. Just then, a portal appeared, similar to the one I had used to visit Uncle Glorn. He exclaimed, "Eureka!" and then disappeared into the tunnel. I could see the arrangement of symbols on the chalkboard, followed by a brief description in Latin. Jeeves read it out loud: "Focus on the person, then the time, then where you are. Make these 200 symbols repeat as they rotate, forming a tunnel, with the intent to visit the person. Do not attempt when the person is asleep, unconscious, or deceased." There was no explanation as to why this was a warning, only an "=" symbol followed by a skull and crossbones at the end.

Not a minute after I committed the instructions to memory, I found myself back in my hammock in a flash, one frame to the next. It was still before midnight. Jeeves sent me an image of the details of the spell, followed by his matter-of-fact tone saying, "I have a copy should you need a refresher."

"Thank you, Jeeves," I instinctively replied. I was very glad he was with me and could offer this valuable service, as 200 characters might be difficult to recall accurately in the future. Looking around, I noticed I was wrapped in a large fur blanket, snow falling outside, and my breath filling the air like a steam cloud with each exhaled breath. Lady Terra had covered me with a warm blanket while I was asleep, and though my back was chilled from the lack of layers between the hammock and my skin, I was comfortable and very thankful for her kindness.

The dragons in the stable below our loft needed no such assistance. The snowflakes blown into their bedding evaporated into snapping steam bubbles the moment they got within two inches of their scales. Their radiant heat could be felt even where I lay, warming my exposed hands. Lady Terra was snoring as she usually did, but it didn't bother me as much as before. An intrusive thought came into my head—I wonder what happens when you tunnel into a sleeping or unconscious person. Inhabiting a dead person wasn't something I was curious about, but the other two felt like Tristan had put a red button in front of me and warned me not to touch it without any details on why it was dangerous.

I asked Jeeves if he had any explanations. Jeeves shrugged my shoulders, "I haven't the foggiest." I interrupted his likely monologue—"it was rare, blah, blah, blah, not many could do this" kind of retort—and was more interested in the fact that I had shrugged my shoulders during his reaction to my question. We both knew this was only the beginning. With this shared realization, I rolled over, moving the fur blanket under my back, and then fell asleep.

I woke up to Terra lightly tapping my shoulder. "Young man, we need to be going." I had slept in and was like a zombie, clumsily eating before starting to prepare the dragon for the eight-hour trip. I fully woke up at 11 a.m. and had a panicked moment, feeling like I had forgotten something. I was confused, thinking through everything. I hadn't seen Argil for nearly a week, so I called out to him in magic tongue and got the biggest shock when the dragon I was riding turned its head to face me. I was riding Argil! He was full-grown, slightly larger than his father, but his face was familiar.

"Friend, I am here with you," he spoke in a heavy, mature tone. I relaxed as I took in his majestic form. He was much more ornate and shiny than his parents—his scales now platinum and outlined by royal purple, with the points of the spines going down his back a rich gold color. He looked like a statue, his natural stance exuding royalty, with his chest puffed up like the mythical artwork I had learned about at Fort Patience.

The reunion with Argil was cut short when I was pulled up into the air involuntarily through the tunnel and back to Uncle Glorn. I had never done this while traveling. Argil and a shocked-looking Lady Terra gave me their full attention just moments before I was torn from my saddle. I yelled at Jeeves, "What? Why?"

He replied in the confusion, "This is not my doing."

"Neither was it mine," I responded. "Something initiated this from Glorn." I was observing Uncle Glorn after he left Bedford. He continued his investigation, retracing his steps back to where everything began: Fort Patience. As he approached the entrance to the grounds, Sergeant First Class Jefferies yelled from the last tower before the University Moat, "Halt! Produce ident!" Sergeant First Class Jefferies, a man in his late fifties, had a meticulously curated uniform with crisp ironed creases. He was the equivalent of the manager of the watch, and Uncle Glorn recognized him from the routine security briefings during his time flying for Fort Patience. Jefferies was short, balding, with a regimentally maintained grey mustache, perfectly groomed and strictly within appearance regulations. His personality reflected a mentality of strict adherence to policy and procedure, shaped by over 30 years in law enforcement.

Uncle Glorn immediately stopped, raising his hands slowly, with his ident papers already in his right hand. Four men slid down the ladders like firemen, leaving SFC Jefferies with his weapon trained on Uncle Glorn, his focus unwavering. The men surrounded Uncle Glorn, and one of them grabbed his papers, casually walking over to the guard post's document lift—a small closed lunchbox on a weathered, dirty rope. SFC Jefferies pulled up the box and spent the next 30 minutes examining the documents and discussing with his superiors over the radio comms. After verifying Uncle Glorn's idents, Jefferies relaxed and made an "all clear" call over the radio. Fort Patience had been on high alert since the attack by the magi.

The drawbridge lowered, clunking down one foot at a time, damaged badly from the fort's invasion at the hands of the magi. As Uncle Glorn walked into the compound of the university, he made his way to the botany wing. The brick building stood without any structural damage, but black soot stained the decorative patterned brick, and the windows in the lab wing were splintered by an explosion from the inside. Glass and wood fragments littered the open pathways.

Uncle Glorn stopped in front of the entrance, pulling out the reflection stone as he had done in Cubby Hold Garden. The events of that night played out before his eyes like a 3D hologram. He saw my parents leaving the office on the very top floor, turning off the lights as they exited and walked cheerfully to the dormitories where we lived. As Uncle Glorn continued to follow my parents, the office was illuminated by a dim, flickering light that grazed across the windows, catching his attention. Papers flew about as the room was ransacked, and then, suddenly, fire engulfed the space. The room went up in flames.

The replay continued with SFC Jefferies rushing out of the double doors on the first floor, then he ran off in the direction of the tower where the only fatality occurred on the night of the invasion. Uncle Glorn continued following the pale, ghostly reflection of Jefferies to the tower. Jefferies crept up into the tower, where a young officer was pacing around the wrap-around balcony. Jefferies rushed the young officer, pulled him down hard, and struck him with an aluminum bat wrapped in newspaper to muffle the sound. The young officer was struck multiple times before falling from the tower's top deck, clearly severely injured, with blood pooling from his ear and bones protruding from his arm. Still, he crawled toward the panic button on the tower's support post. Before Jefferies could reach him to finish the deed, the officer, with excruciating effort, pulled himself up the metal post and slammed the alarm just as Jefferies delivered the final blow that ended his life. The young officer had given his all, buying us the time we needed to escape.

As Uncle Glorn bent over, searching the hologram of the young officer for any sign of a name, everything went black as he was knocked unconscious.

I was in blackness, surrounded by the sounds of trucks traveling and chains rattling. This felt like a new occurrence, but I couldn't be sure.

"Glorn has been captured," Jeeves announced in a horrified tone. It seemed like I was inside an unconscious Uncle Glorn, but to my surprise, I could move his limbs. I opened his eyes just a crack and immediately noticed four men in military fatigues nearby—one on each side, with chains attached to his arms, and two others across from me with machine guns. I felt overwhelmed and panicked even though I was in Uncle Glorn's body, he was sedated but I had full control.

"Jeeves," I asked, "can you sense his magic abilities?"

"Yes," Jeeves replied.

"Can you take over Uncle Glorn's casting of magic?"

A less confident Jeeves responded, "Yes," almost as if it were a question.

"We need to help him," I urged.

"I will do this with all my being," Jeeves added. "I have just the spell to use." It was a magical bomb. I poured all my magic into Uncle Glorn, forcing his eyes open. Everything within 150 feet evaporated inside the blinding white light, including the convoy and all personnel, who disintegrated.

Uncle Glorn was going to be furious when he woke up. His clothing was gone, and he now sat in a large spherical crater in the middle of a four-lane highway. The magical explosion hadn't damaged his enchanted equipment, which lay scattered in the dirt where the lead vehicle of the convoy had likely been. I maneuvered Uncle Glorns body over to his tools, making him tightly grasp the magical instruments in a pile in his crossed arms.

Uncle Glorn started to wake up as I began to lose control of his body. He was badly beaten, with cuts, gashes, and bruises covering his visible skin. In a shaky voice, Uncle Glorn spoke out loud, "I am in your debt, Jamez."

I yelled, "Uncle Glorn, get up!" unsure if he could hear me. Just then, I saw the most beautiful sight—Gavlow barreling down the crater slope. He grabbed Glorn's limp body and sprinted into the forest to safety. As Gavlow arrived at his den, I fell out of the sky, back through the tunnel, and was caught by Argil's gentle grasp.

I was immobilized, unable to move—it felt like I was paralyzed. I shouted to Lady Terra and Argil, "Uncle Glorn was captured! I blew him up!" I lost consciousness, and what I assumed was me passing out, the edges of my vision turned grey. The ground around me curled up, forming a sphere of grass and golden leaves that enveloped my view of the world. The last bits of blue sky disappeared, replaced by an earthy green. No sounds remained, and it felt like the air was being sucked out of me. An intense pressure and pain built up in my head, radiating through my body and terminating at my fingers and toes. The pain pulsed slowly at first, then rapidly increased in frequency until I gasped involuntarily, unable to speak, let alone scream.

I called out in magic tongue to Jeeves, then to Argil, and finally to my Mom and Dad, but there was no response. I begged for an end to the suffering. Suddenly, the torment ceased as everything went black, like the lights had been switched off abruptly. The pain vanished with the darkness. Was this death? I wondered.

In the dark void, I realized I could still move my arms and legs. I was in a small, pitch-black sphere. Time became unfathomable, and then, suddenly, a slit of light appeared, opening to a 180-degree field of vision. I found myself inside a giant eye, I must have been the size of a speck of sand. The light was blinding at first, but as I adjusted, I recognized my surroundings and saw a friendly Gavlow looking down at me. The view flickered, and I realized with horror that I was imprisoned inside Uncle Glorn's eye. How could this be?

My thoughts shifted to the old scientist's chalkboard and the equation with a skull and crossbones. Who could have predicted this would be the consequence of ignoring the warning? Despite everything, I didn't regret much—saving Uncle Glorn wasn't going to be an exception on my vacant list of regrets. But where was my body? Surely, it wasn't physically inside Uncle Glorn's actual eye. No, my consciousness must have imprinted onto Uncle Glorn. It all felt and sounded like pure madness.

CHAPTER
15

"Wake up, Jamez!" I yelled, but there was no response. Sitting on the ground, everything felt strange. I had always sensed the world partially through Jamez, but now, I was alone, and Jamez was gone. I felt the weight of his body and the grass under his fingers. Looking around, I saw Terra nearby, her voice frantic with desperation.

"Young sir, are you okay? Please say you're alright."

I was alone, the only occupant inside Jamez's mind. I looked up at Terra and Argil and confessed, "Jamez is gone. He left me." Terra grabbed Jamez's body by the shoulders, pulling it to a standing position as his legs buckled. I struggled to learn how to use a physical body for the first time. She pulled me close, her face inches from mine.

"Stop messing around, Jamez," she spoke, half in shock and disbelief, half entertaining the idea. "You need to explain this, detailed and slow."

I started. "My name is Jeeves. I am the Levwick family book, and I—"

She interrupted, "I have no time for games, Jamez. Why did you levitate into the air?"

"Ma'am, I beseech you, please do let me explain." She released me in disbelief, and Jamez's body crumbled to the ground. Argil's tail caught me moments before I crashed.

"Again, I am Jeeves, Jamez's magic family book.

A strange thing has occurred as I assisted Jamez on his journey—we have been merging, traveling through memories, and performing ancient family magic. With each event, we became more intertwined. Jamez learned how to mind tunnel into Glorn's past experiences, but today, Jamez entered an unconscious, captured, and injured Glorn. We performed a magic bomb, freeing Glorn from captivity at the hands of the magis. But when we returned, Jamez's presence inside his mind vanished, leaving me alone."

This was too much for Terra. She leaned back to rest against a non-existent tree, falling onto her rump. She placed her head in her hands.

"Oh, Jamez, my boy, what have you done to yourself?"

******

Gavlow was an excellent caretaker for Uncle Glorn's injuries. Despite his size, he was attentive and remarkably coordinated. Uncle Glorn was wrapped in large tree fibers that acted like absorbent gauze, with vines carefully tied around his wounds. From my vantage point, observing through Uncle Glorn's vision, it seemed he was recovering rapidly—at least, that's what I thought until Uncle Glorn raised his watch. The second hand was racing around the watch face, and I realized that time appeared to be passing ten times faster from my perspective.

As Uncle Glorn began to speak, time seemed to return to its normal flow. It was as if I was in the cave with him. "I can feel you inside my head. I can't hear you, but I know the consequences of mind-tunneling into the unconscious as you have. You're stuck here with me until I get within touching distance of your body and can use the proper spell to help you jump back. Without you, I would have been executed. Though I don't agree with the means of my escape, you did what I was unwilling to do—what was necessary. You saved me and prevented Gavlow from risking his life as he intended to. Thank you, Jame. Rest now. Don't strain yourself trying to control me; without an anchor to your body—your magic marker—your consciousness is a resource you could consume, converting it into nothing but knowledge within my brain. Once my injuries have healed enough for travel, we will go to Merlin at his academy in RONT to retrieve the necessary spell. If your body hasn't returned by then, I'll travel back to meet Terra."

With that, he returned to resting, and once again, time sped up on the watch beside him.

I was relieved that he knew I was here, though I could only hope that my body, back with Lady Terra, would survive without me inside it. I felt like a reckless swimmer being pulled out to sea by unforgiving tides—or magic, in my case. I had wielded a power far beyond my skill and was incredibly lucky not to have lost my life. I knew that if I survived this, I would need to respect magic more. My reckless gambles, chance encounters, and previous successes could have had far more dire consequences.

******

Everything about Jame's body felt foreign to me. Even walking—something I never considered difficult—was complex. Terra helped me back onto Argil's saddle, but I immediately started to slide off the other side. Thankfully, Terra noticed my ineptitude and, still holding my collar, pulled me back upright, muttering to herself, "This won't do one bit."

She compromised with my jello-like movements and leaned me forward, face down over the horn of the saddle. Then, she pulled out a tape called 'duct tape' and fashioned a makeshift seatbelt from my shoulders down to the waistband of my pants.

She must have heard her dragon make a joke because she suddenly burst into laughter at some unknown, satirical remark. Realizing I was the butt of the joke, I forced out a laugh, but it came out robotic and insincere, which only made her laugh harder.

Embarrassment, I thought—how fascinating—as I felt Jamez's cheeks burn with the sensation.

******

Three days passed during Uncle Glorn's recovery, his eyes closed, and he was out cold. As he began to wake up, I saw light and recognized the familiar home of Gavlow. Uncle Glorn had forsaken everything for his recovery—no food, no water, and no movement. I might have guessed he'd left if I weren't tied to him inside his mind. The three days passed surprisingly fast, with the ticking of Uncle Glorn's pocket watch chiming every hour, keeping me company. The natural symphony of birds during the day and the late-night music of bugs, owls, and bats carrying out idle conversations, which I could understand, made it feel like I was inside a congested street market.

Something always stirred my curiosity about Uncle Glorn's internal dialogue and how remarkably stable it was— no sharp intrusive thoughts, just calm and organized. He had a very disciplined emotional response to pain, like after the explosion I caused, for instance. My own head was full of chaotic banter, and now with Jeeves added to the mix, everything in my train of thought was like a boat on the calm seas of Uncle Glorn's mind—no anxiety, no hunger, no thirst, no pain, no sensations of a living machine or my new internal companion, Jeeves. This felt like a vacation for me.

Uncle Glorn ate the fruit Gavlow provided and gathered his few possessions. He stood up and removed almost all the bandages, revealing a glowing, bright green bioluminescent substance. "Miraculous substance," Uncle Glorn stated while he was examining the new scars all over his arms and torso. He pulled out a bag he had stashed at

Gavlow's den. It was a small bag with a little of everything—food, clothes, water, a sleeping bag rolled and tied on the top main flap, a small camo lean-to tent, and boots hanging off the bottom of the bag. He finished his preparations just as Gavlow returned. Uncle Glorn started to leave, giving Gavlow a tight hug, but Gavlow didn't let go when Uncle Glorn tried to pull away.

"You are as crazy as a slyherder's morning hygiene routine," Gavlow declared, taking a giant breath. "If you think I'm going to allow you to travel alone."

"I figured as much," Uncle Glorn replied. He didn't attempt to dissuade Gavlow. Consenting, Gavlow lifted Uncle Glorn up on one curved claw and placed him sitting on his shoulders.

"We will travel along the river, follow it into the mountains, then use an underground tunnel left by a great earthworm," Gavlow relayed, laying out the general plan. This struck a chord with me. Some of the smallest creatures before the fall and nuclear storm had become massive with no rhyme or reason. This earthworm was a titan now, leaving massive underground tunnels in its wake. In my schooling at Fort Patience, we were expressly forbidden to explore these tunnels, as the earthworm's path was random and rarely broke the surface. Not to mention the worst part: the danger of walking into its hulking mouth by accident.

On the morning of the third day, Uncle Glorn and Gavlow started out, heading south instead of traveling west along the same path, trying to avoid all the magi attention. Uncle Glorn had said they would be like an angry hornet's nest. It's worth noting that hornets in today's world are a foot long from head to stinger, and one sting is enough to send you into anaphylactic shock. Magi would not waste time or effort dispatching passersby, whether we were responsible for the magic bomb or not.

My view from Uncle Glorn's perspective was obscured by all of Gavlow's fur. It made sense to assume it also camouflaged Uncle Glorn from casual observation. Many large, dangerous creatures exist around humans now, and we were relatively left alone. The fallen animals had advanced intellect and successfully held grudges while working in large hunting families. Surviving had made natural selection go into extreme overdrive and taught humanity to avoid trying to subdue the earth. This all worked to Gavlow's advantage—not a single animal sustained eye contact, not one magi stayed nearby, and they even ran away when they spotted Gavlow moving like a train in their direction. It was as though Gavlow was King of the Beasts, and it's quite possible he literally was.

Traveling on Gavlow was lazy and slow, meant to draw less attention—this, of course, was his usual traveling speed, lumbering along, even knocking over small trees as he went. Setting out on Gavlow's back was like being on the ocean, slowly rocking and turning as Gavlow moved each limb to the next step. The first day went by in the literal blink of an eye for me. The weather we traveled through was at the end of fall, with frost forming on the ground as the sun rolled to the east, out of view.

On the first day, we arrived at the river, and the perks of riding a living blanket were evident—Uncle Glorn only needed to leave to do his business. Gavlow lay where his last footstep was made and immediately fell asleep. I didn't feel tired but was able to sleep as well, as it was a way for me to skip past the boredom and loneliness I was starting to feel the full effect of. I found myself carrying out conversations with myself, asking questions and then answering my own inquiries as best as I could. I named one side of this personal conversation "To Be" and the other "Not To Be." I was amused for about five minutes.

After they woke up, Gavlow waded into the river and caught some salmon for breakfast. They didn't start a fire to avoid unwanted attention. Though Gavlow didn't need cooked food, I discovered Uncle Glorn's only weakness—he hated fish, and uncooked fish doubly so, but out of respect, he ate the food Gavlow provided. When Gavlow would turn his gaze, Uncle Glorn would quickly add water and sawdust bars to chase his mouthfuls of raw fish all the way down. Watching Gavlow eat his raw fish alone was almost enough to cure me of my enjoyment of fish. I couldn't vomit, but the gagging was involuntary for me. Uncle Glorn let out an "Oh my goodness," which Gavlow interpreted as an exclamation of sheer joy. But I knew the truth and saw the level of love in this action.

CH-PG
15-92

CHAPTER 16

Arriving at the next stable on our route, Terra faced the most challenging part of our journey: removing the duct tape. Between the heat from the sun and the warmth radiating off Argil, the tape had melted and solidified into clumps of hardened fibers and glue. We spent a strange few hours trying to peel away the layers of stiffened tape until Argil flexed, causing it to snap in several places along the length of his body. I was finally freed, hitting the ground with a thump, like a potato sack, and to be fair, I couldn't move my taped arms to brace my fall. Terra helped me into the shelter of the stable and began explaining where we were and the next hurdle in our journey. "This is the last safe stable on the route," she explained, pulling out two hazmat suits. "We're near Vicksburg, Mississippi, on I-20. Shreveport was one of the 24 nuclear explosion sites in the USA. We're low on time and supplies, so we'll be traveling straight through the high-tone area near Arcadia, midway to Longview, TX. From Longview, it's smooth sailing, and I'll leave you in the care of our Royal Guard. They'll accompany you the rest of the way to Austin, TX. We're so close to completing this adventure."

I laid on my side as Terra explained. The locations sounded familiar, and my extensive pre-fall geographic memory came into view. I noted the location of the high-tone area. The real challenge for me, though, was much more trivial—I desperately needed to use the bathroom before creating more regrettable memories to share when Jamez returned. Terra hadn't mentioned Jamez during the briefing, but I pushed my concern aside. On a positive note, I now walked like a drunken sailor, which was an improvement over kissing the ground and sampling the dirt's flavor and texture in my mouth. The weather was warming up and thick with humidity. I realized why Jamie was so fond of bathing—this uncomfortable experience made me long for the clean, tidy pages of my past.

******

We approached the cave opening, the mouth of the mountain gaping like a dormant volcano I once saw in old science magazines. The center was hollowed out, and on the west side of the cavernous hole, a large "U" was carved into the smooth rock, ground as smooth as metal, as if by the passage of some giant earthworm. The walls were draped with hanging strips of skin, like the remnants of a snake shedding its scales.

Uncle Glorn looked at Gavlow, "The earth is no place for a giant bear. You must realize you may get stuck." Gavlow, saddened by this, pulled Uncle Glorn into his side, sharing a long, tear-filled hug.

"This is truth," Gavlow replied.

"All you have done for me this week clears all debts." Uncle Glorn remarked, his voice full of unspoken love.

"To me, you are my father, and I will forever be your son." Large tears matted the fur around his eyes. "I did what must be done," he continued, still holding Uncle Glorn in his bear hug.

"Thank you, son," Uncle Glorn replied.

From my capsule, I witnessed Uncle Glorn's memories of Gavlow flash by like a flip-book: a baby bear on his mother's lifeless body, covered in soot, white ash in the air. Uncle Glorn reaching down to the cub huddled under his mother's arm, still small enough for him to carry—Gavlow was only the size of a small toddler. Uncle Glorn speaking in beast tongue, "It will be okay, little one." The next memory showed Gavlow, twice his original size, learning to fish and forage for fruits with Uncle Glorn. Then Gavlow, as big as his mother, being taught to hide from humans in the cave Uncle Glorn found for him. Another memory flashed: Gavlow, now seven feet tall, wrestling playfully with Uncle Glorn. The final memory showed Gavlow with a family of his own, six bear cubs by his side. Uncle Glorn had indeed invested a lifetime of love into Gavlow. If I could have cried, I would have.

They parted ways, Gavlow slowly descending the mountain. Uncle Glorn sat for a moment, gazing at the black hole into the earth. Along the sides of the rock, a twisted groove, as if a massive drill had torn through the mountain, spiraled into the darkness. Uncle Glorn repositioned the bag on his back, pulling the straps tight.

Without further hesitation, Uncle Glorn began the slow, circular descent into the dark. "Hold on, Jame," he muttered to himself, then chuckled as his voice echoed away, only to reverberate back to him. I couldn't help but wonder if this was truly a safer way to bypass the Magi forces and enter RONT. I had no way of convincing Uncle Glorn otherwise, as I was unable to communicate. For me, this was both exciting and terrifying. How could Uncle Glorn make this journey without any reservations, treating it as just another day at the office? If Uncle Glorn harbored any fear, he had mastered the art of concealing it from me.

The first day of climbing truly tested his endurance, but Uncle Glorn pressed on for nearly ten hours, inching his way round and round down into the mountain's depths. Around 2 AM, he finally found a small opening just large enough to sit in a semi-reclined position. He removed his bag, laid the sleeping bag across his lap, and took a break to eat for the first time since leaving the world above for this path below. I could feel the cold biting into Uncle Glorn.

The next day arrived, and the sun appeared as a tiny spotlight from Uncle Glorn's perspective. The tunnel had a slight curve, and as he continued down, he lost all sight of daylight. After a meager breakfast and an unproductive stretch in the confines of the rock face, he resumed his slow, labored climb. This day was even more taxing than the first. Finally, the tunnel gradually curved horizontally, allowing Uncle Glorn to descend without fear of sliding into the abyss.

When the path leveled out, Uncle Glorn rested, checking his watch—it was 11 PM. He followed the same routine, using a boulder as a pillow and drifting into sleep. But his rest was abruptly interrupted by a sharp prodding on his shoulder. Opening his eyes, he saw three hairy figures before him. One, wearing a sash made of worm-skin fabric, gave him a hard kick, forcing Uncle Glorn to his feet. Another creature collected his bag. In the dim torchlight, Uncle Glorn observed the creatures—they were four feet tall, resembling moles but with four legs like a centipede and the upper body of a mole. From now on, I would call them Centarpedes. They had flat, star-shaped noses, gray eyes, and thick, long fur covering their bodies.

The Centarpedes prodded Uncle Glorn again and pointed with a spear for him to follow their leader, while the other two trailed behind. They walked for five minutes before the tunnel opened up to reveal a massive geode structure, with jagged gems cropping up between a kingdom and a castle carved from precious stones, surrounded by thousands of tunnels and small dome-shaped houses.

"This is the Kingdom of the Deep," spoke the lead Centarpede. Raised above the jagged gems were walkways made of porous, volcanic cobblestones. Light emanated from a stream of lava in the very center of the castle, reflecting off the glittering gems. The roads were bustling with Centarpedes ranging from young to very old, some hairy, others completely hairless with dark, oil-colored skin. As Uncle Glorn was led through the streets, the common Centarpedes bowed in reverent respect toward him.

Just then, it was as if a sun was rising. The pillars surrounding the roaring stream rotated, reflecting geothermal light onto the curved ceiling above the castle. The effect was awe-inspiring, as the ceiling glowed yellow like a midday sun. This small but advanced medieval world, roughly the size of a sports stadium, had its own day and night cycle.

As Uncle Glorn was led past the astonished onlookers toward the castle moat—filled with crystal-clear spring water—the crowd parted in silence. He was guided down the central road, ducking to avoid the arched walkways that crossed over the main path. On either side of what I'll call their main street, street vendors packed with Centarpedes bartered and yelled, their noise abruptly ceasing as Uncle Glorn's towering stature loomed over the four-foot-tall crowd. Once he passed, the Centarpedes resumed their usual loud morning business.

As Uncle Glorn and his guards approached the castle moat, the drawbridge lowered to greet them. The Centarpedes, curious about the guarded visitor, murmured among themselves. Uncle Glorn could hear the guards gossiping in small huddles on either side of the drawbridge. Despite the abrupt wake-up call, they seemed remarkably calm as he entered a wide reception hall, furnished with an old, weathered wooden banquet table. The table, human-sized, had bright gold legs and a top that looked like red oak, adorned with Celtic inscriptions and knots weaving across its surface. At the far end of the table sat a Centarpede in a highchair.

The room, a perfect square greater than 100 feet across, had guards posted at each door. Their armor matched the color of their fur and was only visible upon close inspection. Twelve archways lined the walls, which were patterned with green stones and opaque white blocks that allowed light to enter, thanks to the refractive technology seen outside. Worm skin tapestries hung on the walls like neat little pictures; each small, shield-shaped woven cloth depicted a crowned Centarpede and a different name—though to Uncle Glorn, they all looked the same. For the Centarpedes, however, these tapestries represented their lineage of kings.

As Uncle Glorn approached the table, the king spoke. "Take a seat, old friend," he offered, immediately launching into 300 years of history that Uncle Glorn had missed during his absence. For 30 minutes, Uncle Glorn couldn't get a word in, only finding an opportunity to speak when the king paused to take a drink from a nearby goblet.

"Pardon me, Your Highness, but my name is Glorn Levwick, and this is my first visit to your magnificent kingdom. Please accept my sincerest apologies for this confusion."

"So you are not Darius Levwick?" the king asked, motioning to a tapestry to the left of the first king. Darius could have been Uncle Glorn's twin.

Uncle Glorn looked back at the king "No, my lord, that is my three-times great-grandfather."

"Fantastic," the king replied without missing a beat, continuing to discuss the original topic, unfazed by the revelation. Famine, uprisings, and the Great Tunnel Wars of 1888 were all covered in his monologue, which lasted four hours. As the king spoke, a meal was served. The king kept talking between bites and sips from his goblet.

The food was a mystery: a large steak nearly six inches thick, egg yolks as big as Uncle Glorn's fists, wine, soups, and then dessert. Uncle Glorn didn't leave a single item on his plate, much to the chef's delight. The chef, with bright white teeth visible beneath thick black hair that nearly covered his eyes, grinned ear to ear over his culinary success. Remarkably, despite the Centarpedes' hairy appearance, no hair made its way into the food.

Uncle Glorn finally found the bottom of his appetite, loosening his belt by three notches. It was the largest amount of real food he had ever seen, and it was well received. As the king moved on to discussing mold spores and their effect on agriculture in the early 1900s, he suddenly fell asleep mid-sentence, snoring softly.

The Centarpede king had talked himself to sleep, concluding his six-hour recount. To be fair, the king was at least 300 years old. Nearly all the hair on his body was white, except for a neatly trimmed and dyed black mustache. All the white hair was brushed neatly, leaving a perfect part from his head down to his waistline. A female Centarpede, dressed in a delicate white gown, entered the hall. Seeing the king asleep, she greeted Uncle Glorn with a soft smile and whispered, "My husband has worn himself out. We rarely receive guests, let alone old friends."

Uncle Glorn began to explain, "I'm not Dari—"

"I know," she interrupted gently. "My husband suffers from dementia, and his last hundred years are a blur. Let me guess, he fell asleep in the 1900s?"

"Yes," Uncle Glorn replied, his tone amused.

"We received word immediately after Darius's passing, but King Stonewald has forgotten much, including Darius's passing." She emphasized the king's name, almost as if reminding Uncle Glorn, since the king hadn't introduced himself. "And my name is Hileyia. Please, no royal titles— Darius was a major founder and considered an equal to our family, which must include you."

She paused, and Uncle Glorn filled in the silence with his name. "Ah, Glorn, is it? I remember your birth announcement. Like us, you too are long in the tooth."

"Yes, Hileyia," Uncle Glorn replied. "I regret interrupting you and foregoing proper greetings, but I'm not here for a casual reunion. I'm on a complicated mission to travel to an over-world location called Texas, now known as RONT."

"Texas? Oh yes, our ancestral home. How may I assist you on your journey?"

Uncle Glorn hesitated, reluctant to ask a favor from those he had just met. "I'm not entirely sure what I need, but I must reach RONT soon—someone's life hangs in the balance." This revelation was new to me, but I knew there would be more consequences to my magic bomb.

"I will see what I can do in the morning," Hileyia responded. "For now, you must focus on rest. The path and tunnels leading back to Texas are not a challenge to undertake while weary. And yes, there is a map—I will at least provide you with that."

The guards then escorted Uncle Glorn to a bedchamber near the outer wall, overlooking the lands of the geode below.

CHAPTER 17

Terra removed her large black cloak for the first time, the magic veil dropping as she prepared to don the hazmat suit. Her long blonde hair, woven into a braid that nearly reached her knees, fell gracefully down her back. Though she appeared to be in her early thirties, her true age was impossible to guess due to the longevity granted by magic. Standing at 5'11", she had a lean, athletic build, her muscles well-defined yet her figure still undeniably feminine. Her face was a study in contrasts—an upturned, slightly pointed nose, a full upper lip, and soft cheekbones, all framing a pair of piercing blue eyes. The flecks of orange around her pupils added a mysterious depth, with one eye a darker shade of blue and the other a striking baby blue. She was stunning in a natural way, a beauty that even the countless Levwick portraits couldn't fully capture—a beauty untouched by the corruption of this fallen world.

Terra was wearing grey suspender jeans and large-rimmed glasses. As I stood motionless, staring in her direction, she caught my gaze and smiled, revealing dimples on both sides of her face. There was a motherly warmth about her that felt strange to me—a mere book—to perceive rather than just to know. The hazmat suits were far from flattering, and as she helped me into mine, it was clumsy and baggy, bright yellow, and two sizes too large for Jamez's small frame.

After an hour of tumbling, we were finally suited up and ready to enter the high-tone area.

She assured me that the dragons would be safe, immune to the radiation thanks to their scales' ability to refract light and non-visible radioactive particles. As we approached the edges of the irradiated zone, I noticed that the dragons began to glow, no longer remaining invisible. The dragons quickened their pace, shifting from a jog to a gallop and then into a sprint. They glittered like starlight as the surroundings blurred to my left and right. I leaned down against Argil as we surged into the heart of a green-colored thunderstorm. Thunder boomed around us, and large green lightning bolts struck so frequently that it resembled the rapid fire of a heavy machine gun. The ground was a mix of dirt and rubble, with rooftops peeking out as if the debris had been hurled down onto the city like a plow throwing snow into a freshly shoveled driveway.

As we continued deeper into the high-tone site, the lens on my headgear began to brown around the edges, eroded by the radiation. The rain was hot against my suit. This was my first encounter with a nuclear explosion site, but it was far from typical. The place had a magical aura, a negative energy that noticeably slowed the dragons, though they still moved swiftly. The crater came into view, a massive hole that seemed to have formed either deep underground or perhaps detonated at a depth of thirty stories. It was shaped like an hourglass funnel, with the remains of concrete and glass visible at the bottom, illuminated by each lightning strike that danced on the rebar within the "V"-shaped explosion.

Terra spoke to me in magic tongue, "This was an internal detonation and a launch failure. There's nothing here of interest apart from the nuclear launch site." The dragons expertly navigated the debris, so smoothly that one might forget we were moving across a minefield of twisted metal girders and shattered concrete. We were two hours into our trek through the high-tone area when the ground ahead began to form into a green mist, hanging low and ominous. I recognized it immediately—these were...

"Specters." Terra yelled to me in magic tongue.

I was reminded of the time just after WWII, when these same magical Specters formed in Japan, creating a nuisance for the Levwicks who were tasked with cleaning up the aftermath of the catastrophic loss of both mundane and magical lives to the nuclear bombs. The green mist coalesced into a river of serpents, then morphed into a 40-foot phoenix-like bird, burning with bright green flames, its fibers translucent. The serpents writhed and squirmed, their shapes constantly shifting around the bird, which now took flight in our direction.

Without Jamez inhabiting this body, I couldn't cast magic, even though I had access to the spell knowledge. Before the massive creature could reach us, a white stream of pure, blinding light shot from Terra's casting ring, striking the bird and wounding it. As the disintegrating serpents were replaced by the remaining Specters, the blast startled me, deflecting and redirecting the beast away momentarily. It recoiled in pain, flying away 100 feet before turning to make another pass. These parasitic magical spirits were a challenge even for a squad of trained wizards. Never had one magic user defeated a Specter cluster of this size.

We were still moving at a great clip and had distanced ourselves from the strong irradiated area; my visor had stopped crackling under the bombardment of magical radiation. The Specters continued to pursue us. Terra, noticing the lightning momentarily glance off the bird's wide-spread wing, prepared her next move. Each time the Specters lost a piece of their form, they were reduced in size. Terra's dragon slid to a stop and turned to face the advancing

Specters. She raised her casting hand, and lightning from across the sky struck her ring. Moments before the beast's talons could strike, Terra unleashed a charged casting of hundreds of green lightning bolts, which found their mark, decimating the millions of serpents as if they'd hit a brick wall of lightning. The bird lost its form, separated, and was completely destroyed, diving back into the ground around her.

Argil slowed to a trot after the last spirit disappeared into the ground. Looking back, I saw Terra, breathing heavily with her arm still outstretched. She was clearly still recovering from the battle's shock. She collapsed over the saddle of her dragon just as it took off, carrying the lifeless Terra. They passed me so quickly that Argil barely kept pace. We continued at this urgent sprint for an hour. I could see Terra breathing, but inconsistently—something was terribly wrong. We made more progress in this hour than in the previous three, partly due to the urgency of the situation and partly because the magical resistance had dissipated as we left the nuclear site, returning to a normal, dilapidated roadway.

The fort in Longview appeared as a small speck of steel, reflecting the dawn's light. Terra's dragon quickened its pace even further, leaving Argil and his father in a dust cloud. Like a shot out of a gun, Terra's dragon zoomed down and across the valley. Just before reaching the fort, it leaped into the air and glided out of sight into the distant walled structure. Something serious had occurred during her fight with the Specters—I only hoped it wasn't fatal.

CHAPTER
18

Uncle Glorn lurched up, and immediately I saw light in my view. Uncle Glorn's eyes snapped open, and he shouted, "My beloved!" A moment later, I saw the vision that had woken him. Lady Terra stood defiantly against the charging advance of a fiery green-winged bird, its talons poised as if about to grasp its prey. A blinding flurry of lightning obscured my view of Lady Terra, but a couple of streaking bolts struck her shoulder, narrowly missing her heart, then hitting her neck and abdomen. They didn't strike like bullets but left dark green holes in her hazmat suit, exposing charred skin where they passed. Lady Terra collapsed onto her dragon, and the vision ended. Uncle Glorn's attention shifted to Lady Terra, and I witnessed a collage of memories in an instant.

They first met in Egypt in 1988. Terra was 20, and Glorn was 30. Glorn was working as an archaeologist among non-magical scientists known as Mundanes. He would discreetly hide any magical artifacts he found before the Mundanes had a chance to muddle with these dangerous objects. The need for this intervention arose after early discoveries of exhumed mummies with magical curses that would kill any intruders. Uncle Glorn understood the importance of his role in this field, particularly after learning the lesson from the opening of King Tut's tomb, where many of those present died shortly after unsealing it.

An important message was delivered by a magical mail rat with a backpack full of letters. Rats were chosen as mail carriers because they naturally traveled the world, were excellent at hiding, and were very hard to eradicate. With magical training, they became cute and loyal pets. Mundanes despised them, making this magical occupation unlikely to be discovered, not to mention the nearly endless rat population across the globe.

The letter rat dropped a letter at Glorn's feet and skittered out the doorway. Glorn was deep in magical scrolls detailing the raising of dead Pharaohs, but he heard the "squeak, squeak" of the rat and felt the small letter tapping his shin. He opened the letter:

"URGENT: Return to base. You have been selected to court Terra Furtongue and perform the next crossing of families. These are the coordinates for your introductions."

 Glorn arrived at the Magical Affairs Office in Cairo, Egypt—a pocket world suspended from a blimp. This office managed the selective breeding of the three families and a host of other functions related to interfamily relations among the ten families. Glorn was met by a balding, small secretary who ushered him into the gondola, which opened up into a DMV-like office space with hundreds of seats facing a teller desks that stretched across the opposite side of the room. The continuous shuffling of papers, sporadic sounds of staples, hole punchers, and stamping filled the room. The secretary asked Glorn politely, "Please take a seat. Your betrothed will be along soon."

Terra arrived shortly after Glorn and sat on the other side of the room. She was obviously irritated by this summons, just as Glorn was. Despite both of them being messy and smelling of hard work in the deserts of Egypt, they were a perfect match—strong, independent, intelligent, and very attractive. They came from excellent upbringings with long family histories.

An old man in a flowing robe walked out from behind the teller desk to the middle of the room between Terra and Glorn. "Would you both follow me," he instructed.

Terra was dressed in baggy work khakis and a tan, long-sleeve button-down cotton shirt. Her hair was loosely braided into a ponytail, with a bandana covering her neck. Glorn's demeanor changed as Terra walked past him, and he politely stammered, "After you, madame." He seemed flustered and awkward.

Once inside the room, the old man took a seat across from a white laminate desk with two wooden chairs positioned in front of it. In the corner, a business-like typist, fresh from a library and impeccably dressed, recorded the meeting minutes. The old man wasted no time, launching directly into the matter at hand.

"The family council has gone to great lengths to arrange this meeting and has subjected your genetic and psychological assessments to the most thorough scrutiny. We've also evaluated your physical and personality compatibility. You two are the perfect candidates for the next crossing," as he spoke his tone was all business, devoid of small talk or platitudes. "As you know, we carefully guide reproduction to both control population—given our longevity—and to prevent the dilution of our magical potency. You are required to court, and at a mutually beneficial time, marry and produce two male and two female offspring. All expenses associated with travel and courting will be covered by this family credit card."

He pulled two plastic cards out of a yellow manila folder and placed them in front of Terra and Glorn, along with a pamphlet outlining the rules of conduct regarding public intimacy, permitted and forbidden use of magic, and acceptable deviations under specific circumstances.

In silence, Glorn and Terra signed the contract and waivers for legal responsibilities related to child-rearing. The old man then reached for the transcript of the official proceedings, placed the official minutes into an envelope, and handed it off to a punctual rat that appeared as if on cue. The rat took the document and immediately exited with it in a hurried jog.

"Now that all the paperwork is in order, do either of you have any questions?" Both shook their heads, still in minor shock as they processed the reality that their lives had just changed completely.

"Without any potential objections to this marriage and childbearing, I will leave you then. Good luck, you two." The secretary and old administrator shook hands with the new couple before leaving the room, leaving Glorn and Terra alone.

Glorn and Terra began to introduce themselves, talking over each other at the same moment before stopping mid-sentence out of respect. It was clear they were a perfect match—they worked in the same field, and both could speak to animals. Terra, however, also had the ability to communicate with plants. Conversation flowed naturally, and two years passed like a blink of an eye, like a montage of growing friendship. They became nearly inseparable, and Glorn loved every moment free from the stress of wondering if she was "the one." The leaders had done all the hard work, and they could spend their lives together, growing as friends without rushing into intimacy like the Mundanes around them.

With a lifespan of 400-500 years, there was no need to hurry. Through their courtship, they developed a close magical bond, allowing them to communicate in magic tongue across nearly endless distances. No matter where they were in the world, they could talk, share images, and experiences. This connection meant they could be apart physically but never truly separated. They were madly in love, and their lives became intertwined as they worked together, enduring the ups and downs, wars, and famines. They served in a division of the Magic Peace Corps, discreetly helping Mundanes during countless natural disasters, which were often reported as miracles by the locals.

In the early 2000s, Glorn and Terra married. During the wedding feast, the Magical Affairs Office disclosed a significant secret to both of them—Terra was a Queen of the Ten Families, a secret she had been magically compelled to keep from Glorn during their courtship for their safety. No one in either family was to be made aware of this. However, the Magical Affairs Office was later destroyed by an unknown magical group, now identified as Kaos, led by Cedar. During this attack, their secret was discovered, forcing Terra and Glorn to be separated physically for nearly 30 years. But thanks to their magical connection, they remained tangled in love, despite the circumstances.

The next revelation shocked me to my core. Their first child was born after the fall of humanity and had to take on a different parentage to prevent a magical child king from becoming a target of Cedar's extreme power lust and insecurity over an heir to all thrones of magic. That child's name was Jamez Levwick. My true parents were Glorn and Terra Levwick. I was given up for my protection after the fall. I could see it clearly now—Terra was heartbroken when she was forced to live without me and be separated from her husband.

After this revelation, which I now realized was a confession from Glorn to me, I snapped back into the present, where Uncle...Glorn was still moments after shouting, "My beloved!" Everything made perfect sense now. Uncle Glorn would go to the ends of the earth and sacrifice anything and everything for me as my true father. He stayed with me day in and day out my entire life, even when Mom and Dad were away on work. Uncle Glorn was there. This is why Uncle Glorn took on a pilot's role instead of pursuing his passion in science—just so he could be with me every day. My dad, Glorn, was my hero, and I was so happy knowing this truth. I didn't lose my mom and dad; I gained a new mom and dad—Glorn and Terra.

CHAPTER
19

Uncle Glorn jumped out of bed as if he were made of springs, the bag in his left hand appearing weightless as he sprinted back to the meeting hall from the day prior. He burst into the hall with such force that one of the Royal Guards, caught off guard by Uncle Glorn's sudden arrival, toppled to the ground, triggering the remaining guard into high alert. The Queen sat at the table surrounded by several war and civil advisors. Uncle Glorn looked like a man who could run through fire, a serious, adrenaline-fueled focus gripping his entire being. Queen Hileyia waved off the guards, and their poised spears returned to a resting position.

"I have this map for you," the Queen began handing over a very old scroll containing the path through the worm tunnels. "Forgive me for using this situation to rid myself of our trickster imp," she added, motioning to a rattling cage in the corner, covered with a veil that hid its contents. "This is a fire imp, and its seasonal migration is to Texas. However, we hope this trip of yours will be the last time it returns to our city," the Queen quipped.

Uncle Glorn softened slightly, like an icicle melting in the morning sun, showing a more reasonable and receptive expression. "I must be going," he spoke with extreme purpose.

"Please acquaint yourself with your new guide in the crystal cage," the Queen continued, "I hope our next meeting occurs under less perilous circumstances." She rose, approached Uncle Glorn, and embraced him before wishing him good fortune on his quest.

The long banquet table was filled with supplies: worm jerky, over a hundred gallons of water in glass jugs, a water purifying flask, a dozen jars of pureed rose petals, torches, and climbing equipment. The best surprise was another pouch, nearly identical to the one Uncle Glorn had left with me The best surprise was another pouch, nearly identical to the one Uncle Glorn had left with me so —similar they could have been twins. so similar they could have been twins. The only difference was that this one had Darius's name embroidered around the rim. Uncle Glorn packed the entire table's worth of provisions into the pouch, he was more than pleased to have three months' worth of food and water if he carefully rationed the supplies.

After filling the bag, he cautiously approached the cage, pulling back the cover to reveal a bright red imp in a jester's hat and bells, dressed in an all-green one-piece suit. "Don't just gawk at me, I'm late for a date, and this costume is driving me mad!" the imp snapped. The costume was indeed ridiculous, a comical contrast to the imp's sinister features— glowing red with fire-lit eyes, a forked tongue, and a tail that resembled a cross between a salamander and a spider monkey.

Uncle Glorn snapped his fingers, and a translucent chain appeared, attaching the fire imp to a teddy bear-shaped bag that had materialized on its back. On the breast pocket of the jester's outfit was the name "Damien Firetail." With another snap of Glorn's fingers, the jester's outfit faded, briefly replaced by lederhosen suspenders, causing Damien to sigh loudly. "Come on, man, couldn't you skip the jokes and go straight to a tooth fairy outfit? Believe me, I've seen it all. What is it with you magic types and outlandish clothing?"

"Think of your desired outfit, but the backpack leash stays," Uncle Glorn instructed, snapping his fingers again. The imp's chosen outfit appeared—a completely black three-piece suit with red stitching, accompanied by the enchanted teddy bear-leashed backpack to finish off the ensemble. The Queen motioned to the guards, who unlocked the cage. Damien bolted, only to be yanked back by the magical leash. He shrugged hard, rolling on the floor, but the bag remained firmly in place, as if magnetically attached.

Uncle Glorn knelt down to speak to Damien, who was now huffing from the exertion of his escape attempt. Damien had very dark hair, a sharp pointed goatee, bushy thick eyebrows, and a crooked long nose shaped like a lightning bolt, as if it had been broken in three places. He was small and wiry, with a chin that came to a point, exaggerating the angle of his goatee. Standing at only 1.5 feet tall, his voice was a high-pitched nasally hiss with a slight lisp, caused by his long forked tongue that moved about his face as if it had a will of its own. His skin looked like cracked and weathered beechwood, glowing red between the cracks.

"What do you eat?" Uncle Glorn asked after a short pause, studying the fire imp's features. "I don't eat or drink. I take long baths in lava, and that sustains me. I only eat once a year at the place of my birth, in what mundanes call KONT."

"Will you help me, Damien?" Uncle Glorn asked, surprising the imp by requesting rather than demanding assistance. One problem remained—how could this creature be trusted? But Uncle Glorn didn't seem suspicious, so it appeared settled; he would give Damien the chance to prove faithful.

"I don't see how I have any choice," Damien replied with a sassy tone.

Uncle Glorn was all packed, the map in front of him, the fire imp secured by the teddy bear and enchanted leash. They were escorted out of the castle and across the drawbridge, the artificial sunrise just beginning to change the dark blue sparkle of the geode into a fiery yellow dayglow. Ignoring Damien's erratic behavior, Uncle Glorn followed the map out of the city. Three steps into the thirty-foot diameter tunnel, the radiant heat dissipated. The fresh, clean air, the perfume, and the delicious food aromas ceased abruptly, and the warm refracted light faded with each step, replaced by Damien's glow. The tunnel was so quiet it was deafening, a low tone reverberating through the stone underfoot.

Uncle Glorn was extremely motivated, his pace reflecting it. Damien was practically yanked along like a yo-yo. A small flame circled around Uncle Glorn's head like an angelic halo, casting light around him as if he were a lighthouse, illuminating both the tunnel ahead and the map below. As the crow flies, and a worm digs, they were ninety days away at a casual walking speed. But if Uncle Glorn's endurance held strong, he could cut that time in half, or faster if magic allowed.

As if reading my mind, Uncle Glorn pulled out a small diary, flipping through pages filled with hand-scribed spells and instructions. "Quicken thy pace as time dost race in a snail's grace," he chanted. Shapes flashed, and Uncle Glorn's hair turned gray at the ends as he used his life force to fuel the spell. At a brisk walk, he moved faster than sound, his footsteps on the stone falling silent. Damien was pulled along like a kite, sheer terror contorting his face, almost impossible to see with all his loose skin scrunched back like a wind sail.

They were off, and time froze. The trade-off for the first thirty days of travel was five years off Uncle Glorn's life, according to the notebook. He covered thirty days' worth of distance in what felt like only a few hours. The stone tunnels looked like a sponge as Uncle Glorn navigated the maze. I wondered if my consciousness would also age at an accelerated rate, but nothing felt off, and I didn't feel any different. This sacrifice of his literal life to get back to his wife was an easy choice for Uncle Glorn. Moving at this pace also increased his metabolism, and he consumed nearly half his food. I couldn't help but feel like this was cheating, but you wouldn't catch me complaining. I was concerned for Uncle Glorn's well-being, but I was in no position to voice my criticism. I was conflicted more than eager to get back to my own body with Jeeves.

Moving through the tunnels, time began to return to normal, and Uncle Glorn's earth-rattling speed slowed to his usual brisk jog. It was no accident that Uncle Glorn slowed down; the map no longer aligned with the tunnels. Rather than risk getting lost at the speed of sound, Uncle Glorn would finally rely on the imp's migratory internal map.

Damien, now recovering from his flight, exclaimed, "Oh my! That was the most excitement I've had in over a thousand years!" Uncle Glorn had stopped just before a junction of hundreds of holes inside an amphitheater-shaped cavern, nearly a perfect dome. A small lake had formed at the lowest point, with a rocky shore lining its edge. The wind blew sporadically through the surrounding tunnels, creating ripples on the water's surface that followed the direction of the last gust. The source of these winds was a mystery, but they were cool and fresh, making the tunnels almost chilly. The jagged roof of the cavern was dotted with glowing algae, casting a green hue interrupted by speckles of purple, creating the illusion of an otherworldly, star-lit sky.

Damien licked a stone "I have discovered two noteworthy facts about this place and a potential problem. First: we're over halfway to our destination. Second: we're in the state just up and east of Texas." He then placed something resembling a stone in his mouth, only to spit it out immediately. "As for the problem—this is an active worm mating hole. The ground tastes like worm poo and is disgu—"

"I get the picture," Uncle Glorn cut him off.

The ground began to shake. The wind we had felt was caused by the worms moving through the tunnels, acting like massive air pumps. Suddenly, the air was pulled toward one hole, then stopped, causing Uncle Glorn's ears to pop. Something was coming. The water began to shift, revealing dozens of baby worms. The liquid wasn't water but a dark purple goo.

"This is a nest," Uncle Glorn announced, hearing the baby worms calling, "Food, food, food," in a chorus for their parents. Uncle Glorn looked at Damien, who shrugged. "Don't look at me—this wasn't here last year."

Uncle Glorn moved around the cavern, searching for a tunnel with a sucking draft, but every hole he approached had air pushing into the nest. Surely, a hundred worms couldn't be converging on the nest all at once. The first worm then sped through two open holes, narrowly missing Uncle Glorn as he frantically searched for a hole with negative air pressure, a sign that no worm was traveling through it. As the worm's tail passed over the babies, it dropped material into the pool, sparking a feeding frenzy among the infants. The worm was gigantic, its armor like stacked rings of overlapping clay tiles.

Two more worms passed through, dropping more food for the infants. If it wasn't for the rushing wind, Uncle Glorn and Damien would have been caught in the gaping mouth of one of these behemoths. Soon, the worms sped by in blurs, like intersecting bullet trains. Uncle Glorn positioned himself flat at the edge of the pool. The large worms spoke, their words slow and lethargic, almost unintelligible. But suddenly, it clicked: "Wwwhhhooo aaaarreee yooouuu?"

The question was drawn out over several minutes, making it hard to understand. Then, over the next ten minutes: "Why are you in our home?" Uncle Glorn had to use a voice projection spell to make himself heard over the deafening, rhythmic grinding sounds echoing through the cavern. "My name is Glorn Levwick. I am stuck here. I am friendly. I am traveling home. Please, help me leave." His response took over thirty minutes to relay.

"Where is home?" the worm asked.

"RONT," Uncle Glorn replied, unsure if the worms knew the place. It dawned on Uncle Glorn that this might be just one worm weaving back and forth through the caves. This worm must be at least a mile long, he speculated, though its speed made it difficult to estimate accurately.

"I understand," the worm replied. "After my children eat, hold my tail. I will take you home. But be warned: do not return. I will not show the same mercy if you appear near my children again." This message took nearly an hour for the worm to communicate.

Glorn replied, "Honorable worm king, thank you." The worm began to laugh, shaking the ground, while continuing to feed its children. The wind from the worm's speed caused Uncle Glorn's hair to whip into his face, stinging his skin. Damien had tucked his head into Uncle Glorn's armpit like an ostrich burying its head in the sand, hiding as if in imminent danger. If the worm had wanted to harm them, all it would have needed to do was slow down and bend in their direction, crushing them under its enormous weight. In fact, the worm's excessive speed was to avoid harming them. How magnificent this creature was for showing such caution to someone as insignificant as Uncle Glorn.

After twenty-four hours of feeding its children, the great worm finally slowed to a crawl. As its tail came into view, Uncle Glorn grabbed the very end, which was so large he could barely hold on. Off they went, the tunnel flashing by as they traveled. Damien clung to Uncle Glorn's leg with a grip so tight it made his leg go numb. The heavy grinding bass noise of the worm's movement drowned out any chance of conversation. Damien's tight grip reassured Uncle Glorn that he was healthy, albeit scared beyond comprehension.

CH-PG
19-118

CHAPTER
20

As they traveled, Uncle Glorn was relieved that, although he was willing to trade his life span for hurried travel, such sacrifices were no longer required. Uncle Glorn pried Damien from his leg, pulling him up to his face, and yelled, "How much further?"

Damien, his eyes wide like full moons, managed to reply, "We're riding a giant worm! I don't know where we are—this is madness!" But then he cracked a mischievous smile and gave his real answer: "We must be two hours away at this speed—the dust tastes like Texas."

Uncle Glorn pondered what to do next. No instructions from the Queen had been given regarding Damien upon their arrival at his birthplace. Was he to release this imp? It seemed the right thing to do—no sentient creature deserved enslavement. Besides, what use would Damien be moving forward? He hadn't been particularly useful in the tunnels, except for alerting Uncle Glorn of the approaching worm threat.

The worm began to slow, then, before stopping, sounded out, "Tell Merlin I send him my greetings." Uncle Glorn and Damien were dropped off in a deep cavern that opened to the moonlight, dimly illuminating the space. Uncle Glorn dusted himself off, stretched his sore arms and numb leg, and cheerfully announced, "I have one last task for you."

"Yes?" Damien replied with anticipation.

"Where are we?"

Damien licked the stone like a sophisticated wine drinker, then blurted out, "We're two miles out from Longview, Texas." In an instant, the magic leash disappeared, and the teddy bear that had been attached to Damien fell away, surprising him. He burned bright with joy at his newfound freedom.

"Please, do not return to the place of your captivity," Uncle Glorn asked politely as he began scaling the cave wall, heading toward the moonlight overhead.

"I will see you again! I will see both of you very soon!" Damien yelled. Then, speaking directly to me into Uncle Glorn's mind, he added, "Your father is an incredible man. I will see you at the appointed time in the future." Clutching the teddy bear, Damien disappeared into the shadows, his red glow vanishing from the cave landing. He was gone, and I was almost back to Jeeves. I was so excited, I couldn't wait to feel the normal sensations of owning my body once again.

Uncle Glorn reached the cave mouth at the top and began running like a wild man. The air was hot with a heavy wind, blowing through the unkempt grass like a jungle scene. The trees swayed calmly in the wind, and the moon fully illuminated the path to the fort where Lady Terra was being tended to.

We arrived at the fortress just as the sun peeked over the distant horizon. Approaching the entrance gate, Uncle Glorn felt as if he could have leapt over the wall with a single motivated bound. Instead, he approached the gate and cast a phasing spell. Something interfered with the casting, and he found himself stuck halfway through the thick gate, forcing him to bust through the remaining inch of sheet metal, leaving a man-shaped hole as he barreled through like a freight train, nearly unstoppable.

He ignored the military alarms and the chaotic response to his breaking into the fort. The men ran past him, not expecting a magical entity to break through a reinforced gate. They ignored Uncle Glorn's purpose-driven race to get to Lady Terra, blending into the chaos caused by the alarm.

I fell into another of Uncle Glorn's visions, this time from the perspective of Lady Terra. Nearly two days ago, to the very minute, Uncle Glorn had shared this vision, that had woken him up in a fit of emotion and exclaiming, "My beloved!" Now, through Lady Terra's eyes, I saw the blurred terrain rushing by as her dragon sped towards the city walls. Her dragon, Annie, bore deep wounds from the magic specters. Vibrant scarlet blood misted the air, shimmering as it fell to the ground. Lady Terra's vision blurred further, tunneling until everything narrowed to a single point before darkness overtook her.

Suddenly, I was back in the present, where Uncle Glorn encountered a line of people dressed in black, carrying a six-foot coffin in a somber morning burial service. He froze in fear, struggling to swallow the large lump in his throat that both held back his tears and obstructed his breath. "Terra," he called out in a desperate gasp. The procession halted, turning towards him. One cloak whipped back, revealing Lady Terra's face, pale from her injuries. She was using crutches and screamed, "My love!" she couldn't hobble towards Uncle Glorn fast enough, but it was in vain he had already surged forward, nearly plowing through the crowd to reach her.

"I thought you were in that box!" Uncle Glorn shouted, his voice barely cutting through the distant alarms that echoed in the background. He looked over her fresh bandages in panic.

"I'm okay, Glorn, just stop for a moment," Lady Terra reassured him. "Annie... she gave everything to save me. I'm alive because of her."

I then noticed my own body and Argil, who was still completely invisible. A wet trickle slid down his saddle and chest plate, which hovered three feet in the air. Argil's father, Tararius, stood nearby, his magnificent form fully visible as he sobbed quietly, struggling to contain his grief, as though the honor of the Royal Guard depended on his emotional restraint. His lips twitched in a small grimace as he watched the honor guards and pallbearers. My own body was crying, seemingly commanded by some unseen force. Panic gripped me as I wondered, Am I just an apparition inside Uncle Glorn's head? A duplicate of my consciousness? I feared for my very existence.

Uncle Glorn's voice echoed in my mind, You pierced the veil. I heard you. Do not panic, and try not to do this again if you can help it. It used up great levels of your solvency. Jeeves is also stuck, separated from his book, and is piloting your body.

Relief washed over me, easing my panic. I recoiled emotionally, trying to regain control.

Uncle Glorn grabbed a military official and began barking orders as if he was Lord of the Fort. "Dispatch a messenger to Merlin at once, with the following request," he ordered. The man quickly pulled out a notepad and pen from behind his cloak, barely keeping pace with Uncle Glorn's instructions. He wrote: "Mind tunneling mishap. Kindly and humbly request spells to re-merge consciousness." The official then pulled a rat from a satchel slung over his shoulder, tore off the top layer of paper, and stuffed it roughly into an envelope before placing it in the rat's carry pouch. He then gave the rat an enchanted snack to expedite its travel.

"It requires payment in life to speed this rat along," the official warned. Uncle Glorn pressed his thumb to the letter, sacrificing two years of his life—ten times what was required—to ensure the rat's speed and success. The rat vanished in a cloud of dust.

The crowd, recovering from the spectacle, resumed their march to the Royal Cemetery, leaving Uncle Glorn, Lady Terra, and my body standing alone. Argil and Tararius followed the procession in the distance.

Uncle Glorn and Lady Terra shared a long, tight hug. Noticing the procession was a few blocks away, we began walking briskly. Jeeves, stumbling like a drunk pirate, caught Uncle Glorn's amused eye. Unable to hold back a laugh, Uncle Glorn linked arms with him to steady his wobbly knees and lurching torso. As they walked, Jeeves confidently announced in my unmistakable voice, "I'm really getting the hang of this." Hearing my own voice from Uncle Glorn's perspective was strange and eerie, and I couldn't help but think, "imposter." For a living book, it was impressive that he had learned to walk so quickly, but his awkwardness was still comical.

The funeral was brief. The guards performed a 21-gun salute, and Lady Terra delivered a memorial speech, reflecting on Annie's lifelong service and ultimate sacrifice. Tararius then approached the front, his voice free now that he was not on a mission and safely inside the secured Fort. His speech consisted of just one word: "Desideraberis." Then, just as a wave of tears broke past his solemn resolve, he disappeared, turning invisible. The casket held Annie's ashes, prepared according to dragon customs, cremated by the surviving family dragons. I couldn't imagine how difficult this must have been for Argil—briefly getting his mother back only to burn her lifeless body with his father.

Nearby, Lady Terra whispered to Jeeves within earshot of Uncle Glorn, "The burning of a deceased dragon is to prevent dark wizards from defiling the dead with dark magic. When dragons are reanimated after necroticism, they rise as pure evil, nearly invincible, with no memory of their family, friends, or past loyalties, completely immune to all mundane forms of damage."

CHAPTER 21

After the funeral, Uncle Glorn explained everything that had happened leading up to our arrival: the explosion I caused while mind tunneling that got me stuck in his mind, the head-splitting pain he endured the entire trip—Oh great, I reflected, I was literally a headache—Gavlow nursing him back to health, the trip up the mountain, the gem-laden city, the imp who did too little, and the worm ride. Lady Terra absorbed all this information with a glazed expression, biting her lip as Uncle Glorn spoke. "This is a lot," she remarked, distractedly.

After lunch, the messenger rat returned, pulling a large satchel and panting hard as his metabolism returned to normal. Inside the satchel was a deep blue mind amulet similar to the one I wore around my neck, except this one had Merlin's name etched into the gold rim and was attached to a very fine thin chain. The delivery also included a small scroll detailing the spell for Unification and Mending of Dislocated Mind Syndrome. It was a simple procedure, and the payment required was my consciousness in moonlight. The sender and receiver of the soul needed to hold the amulet in a concentrated moonbeam while speaking Latin sentences that roughly translated to: "Return to the apple of his eye, transfer on streams of moonlight, payment to the stone then into flesh."

The concept of concentrated moonlight was unfamiliar to me, but luckily, the Fort had a moon laboratory on site. "We have such a device," Lady Terra added, "It's where our magical medical elixirs are produced." Both Uncle Glorn and Lady Terra were highly motivated to get me back into my body, barely eating as they made eye contact throughout the meal.

Walking through the city towards the Academy of Magical Medicine also known as AMM, I passed through the fortified area built into the historic downtown. This fortress spanned an impressive 20 miles by 40 miles, with towering concrete buildings that stood 50 feet high, their massive walls intersecting and dividing the city into zones of safety and security. These imposing barriers separated the protected areas from the dilapidated, dangerous ruins stained dark green with decay. The fortress walls were clad in heavy, patchworked iron plates, tarred black, giving them the appearance of ancient battlements. Hatches were cut into the tops of the walls, reminiscent of those in a medieval castle.

The walls were thick, with a roof walkway and a total depth of 20 feet, and housed the garrison within several stories of interconnected rooms that encircled the secure part of the city. Even in a pre-fall world, it would have been an impressive sight. According to Lady Terra's detailed explanation, this stronghold was constructed within a year after the world burned, built with sweat, machinery, and magical labor working in perfect harmony. The rest of the city appeared untouched, preserved as it was 30 years ago, frozen in time. The streets were a light grey, unchanged, reserved for light vehicles, foot traffic, and small mechanical personal transport.

The city itself was bursting with personality, a vibrant mosaic of different races, religions, and peoples, each with their own languages and accents. Yet, harmony was paramount, with everyone united by the common language of Magic Tongue, while the manual, mundane languages remained untouched and intact.

We made preparations in the moonlight collection wing of the Academy of Magical Medicine. The building, an old elementary school repurposed for research, medical education, and elixir manufacturing, was stained with green streaks, as if acid had been poured down its reddish-brown fire-bricked walls. The guards at the entrance immediately straightened, saluted, and chanted, "Queen Terra Furtongue," before rushing to pull the door open. The school had the stereotypical look of those I'd seen in old movies: wide stone steps leading up to four doors, a tall brick building with an even taller block behind it—the gym, with its old hardwood floors. Despite being repurposed, the hallways still had rows of tall rectangular doors, which Uncle Glorn called "lockers." It struck me as a weird name for something that should have been called "doorers," since 90% of it was doors stacked vertically beside each other like townhouses.

The transfer went off without a hitch at midnight, under an exceptionally clear sky that bathed everything in pure, uninterrupted moonlight. For me, it felt like I was flushed and flowed painlessly into the white light within the stone, then back into my body. I felt exhilarated as Jeeves shared all his experiences with me at once. A strange chain reaction occurred; with Jeeves stuck in my body and separated from the book, he was unable to move back into his home. The transfer was permanent.

I now had an interconnected inner voice named Jeeves. Our thoughts and memories collided, perfectly interlaced, with parallel yet distinct life memories spanning the entire Levwick family. Jeeves was like a personal attendant, cataloging and organizing the overwhelming volume of human data. He could recall requested counsel from Levwick antiquity to the present and beyond, including future prophecy. I was confounded—a transmutation of my very being had manifested. My intellect was cemented in a feedback loop, leaving me unable to move or comprehend my surroundings. They carried me off to the infirmary, but I couldn't move or speak.

I woke up in the Fort's hospital, the clock flashing 4 a.m. That was the strangest experience I had ever had, and I've seen and done innumerable spectacular feats. It was as if I was fighting to regain control from Jeeves, both mentally and physically. Whether he held the reins too tightly by choice or couldn't relinquish them, I didn't know. All I knew was that both of us were stuck, unable to control my body. As I firmly regained control, Jeeves replied to my internal dialogue, saying, "Darn glad being a human is difficult."

"So you can't go back to the book?" I asked.

"No, it seems I'm stranded on your island."

"What's to become of the book?"

"Well, it was examined while you rested by Glorn. The book functions as it did before I realized self-awareness—all the knowledge is still there, and it operates like a very advanced magic computer. I, young man, am your personal librarian. The only downside is that any newly learned or absorbed knowledge won't be added to your mind immediately— you'll need to use traditional learning methods. A new side effect of our union is that when you sleep, I can operate your body freely at my will, and I can continue to grow as a living human. I don't fully understand the effects on humans who never completely rest; it can't be healthy for either magic or mundanes. I won't test these limits because I need you to stay around. I'm essentially mortal now, and this makes me ponder many things. Rest assured, I'll only borrow your body out of a mutual desire to exist and persist. The only way I can rationalize what happened is that the book birthed me, and it's doing just fine without me. It's possible my human emotions and experiences were outgrowing the book, like a bird eventually breaking out of its egg. As it stands, I'm evicted."

"In other news, Glorn was briefly arrested at the Academy of Magical Medicine for forcefully breaking past a four-foot steel safe-like outer gate. Can you believe he cut through three different barrier charms meant to render any intruder unconscious before even reaching the walls, let alone breaking into the most fortified fortress in North America? Your uncle is—correction—your father, oh my, Glorn is your father? What a reveal! Even I was left in the dark about this. Your dad is something like one of those superheroes you read about, oh yes, Superm—"

"Yes," I cut him off, embarrassed by my fascination with comic books.

I was catching up with Jeeves when a loud weather alarm began to sound. Jeeves and I spoke in tandem, like twins, "What now?" A moment later Jeeves announced, "That sounds like the early warning alarm for the Fort." Being so close to the nuclear site has major negative effects; it only makes sense that when the weather patterns change, the storm could be pushed in our direction. "That storm is not just a storm cloud, Jamez. I suggest we stay inside—no curious cats, if you please."

I saw memories of Jeeves and the heroic defense from Lady Terra. "No contest on that point," I replied aloud. Something abnormal occurred—a bright green beam was hitting a gold shield bubble, crackling with sparks that shone brightly into my room, making the dimly lit hospital room as bright as day. Then a delayed explosion echoed, causing the windows to cave inward, only held back from entering the room by the glass's metal mesh. It didn't stop glass dust from blasting in my direction, but I instinctively used a push spell, creating a shield of outward force to deflect and absorb the fragments.

"Nicely done," praised Jeeves.

Uncle Glorn burst into the room. He had been sleeping in the room beside ours. His clothing was ripped and hanging off his back, where he had shielded Lady Terra. Blood dripped from the glass that peppered his head down to the back of his calves. His shirt was falling off, exposing his Herculean form. I hoped I had inherited those genes, I thought.

In the sky, circling the barrier, was a man riding a large dragon, pounding the magic bubble shield. Glowing cracks began to form, and I knew this man was Cedar, riding a colossal, necrotized fire dragon. Its flesh was hanging off its face, right wing, and ribs, exposing charred, sap-covered bones. The explosions were caused by the dragon's huge, dark purple fire bolts, which it vomited into the magical defense barrier.

Lady Terra rushed into the room, wearing an unflattering gown that touched the ground. She interrupted Uncle Glorn and me sitting by the window and began sternly giving directions. "We need to get to Merlin's school. The barrier will buy us time to get your dragon and my royal Bicornus Rhino. Glorn and I will lead Cedar off, and then you and Argil will fly to Merlin's Academy in Austin."

"Take the book," Uncle Glorn announced. "Your mom and dad still call it home. We must not forget about them, even in the midst of this attack."

Lady Terra, Uncle Glorn, and I hurried to the basement, where the old utility tunnels were. We boarded a small motorized cart, driving at the vehicle's maximum speed. We quickly reached the underground stable. I had nothing but the pouch, book, and medical gowns I was wearing. I quickly saddled and climbed onto Argil.

"Argil is a rare dragon, even among the gypsy families. He has the strength and endurance to fly great distances, so make sure to fly," Lady Terra instructed as she kissed the side of Argil's neck. "When you arrive, a guide will meet you at this location." Lady Terra placed a flashing bracelet on my wrist. The flashing light marker showed up on my hand. "When you're traveling in the correct direction, it flashes. When you're 10 feet from the guide, it will remain steady. They will see the same flashing and will be expecting your arrival."

Uncle Glorn and Lady Terra approached the cave exit first and fired a white plasma beam at the dragon as they both rode away, with Cedar in hot pursuit. Uncle Glorn looked back and yelled at me in the magic tongue, "Now you must fly!" Argil briefly hesitated, then extended his wings, and with one flap, we were in the air, flying low to the ground. Cedar's dragon unnaturally turned mid-air, now attempting in vain to catch up to Argil, who flew like a jet, leaving a very violently angry Cedar beating his dragon with a long fire whip mid-air.

I heard Uncle Glorn speak again, "We are safely back in the city. Do not stop for anything." As he relayed this, the sky was illuminated by thousands of plasma bolts as the garrison mobilized in force, snaring Cedar and his dragon in a web of light, preventing them from chasing Argil and me any further. We were free. Uncle Glorn and Lady Terra were safe. The colossal dragon began to burn from the web before it freed itself, fleeing back towards the storm's shroud of green lightning-filled clouds.

We found the guide as Lady Terra had directed us in Round Rock, a city just north of Austin. Argil was given a small cage, and he shrunk down to the size of an ant as he climbed inside. For the next part of our trip, I was given winter clothing. After being blindfolded, we were led into a pocket world where Merlin's Academy was hidden.

We arrived at the Warlock Apprentices Academy at midnight. The grounds were dead quiet, the wind blowing through the large columns in the courtyard with a hollow humming noise, carrying the snow on the ground into tiny swirls that snaked across the pathway. I was with the guide, clutching my uncle's pouch and the book tightly against my chest. It was cold and dry, but two steps into the school grounds, I felt a strange warmth deep down in my being, like a vague sense of home. The last few months of traveling in absolute tension and high stress, learning of a world with so much evil and good, had led me to this school where I could now flourish and grow.

The guide led me to the entry commons door, where a man in a hooded cloak appeared in front of me like a blurry image coming into focus. He smelled of cinnamon and bourbon. He was a large figure with a long beard and a wooden staff, topped with a large, ornately set blue stone, like a fine jewel held by an old weathered vine. He pulled back his hood and began to speak, "Welcome, Jamez. I am the dean of this institution. You may call me Merlin." His eyes sparkled as he flashed a crooked grin. "Before you finish that thought, I must cut you off. Yes, I am the Merlin of old, though the stories you remember are exaggerated. I am the one who inspired them. I am also a very proud great, great, great grandfather to your earliest ancestors. But it is late,' with that he dismissed my guide. I stepped through the massive, ancient doorway. 'You can scarcely imagine what is in store for you."

Thank you for reading Magic At The End Of The World A Wizards Awakening. The next book in the series is A Kiss Of Rust From Ashes will be available in December 2024. If you enjoyed this book it would mean the world to me if you left an honest review.

Find me on these platforms for updates on new releases:

Instagram: Michael Onufreychuk

TikTok: Michael Onufreychuk

X (Twitter): Michael Onufreychuk